Mills

BEST SELLER ROMANCE

A chance to read and collect some of the best-loved novels
from Mills & Boon—the world's largest publisher of
romantic fiction.

Every month, four titles by favourite Mills & Boon authors
will be re-published in the *Best Seller Romance* series.

A list of other titles in the *Best Seller Romance* series
can be found at the end of this book.

Sara Craven

PAST ALL FORGETTING

MILLS & BOON LIMITED
LONDON · TORONTO

First published 1978
Australian copyright 1978
Philippine copyright 1978
This edition 1984

© Sara Craven 1978
ISBN 0 263 74738 7

Set in Linotype Plantin 10 on 10½ pt.
02—0684

Made and printed in Great Britain by
Richard Clay (The Chaucer Press) Ltd,
Bungay, Suffolk

CHAPTER ONE

JANNA PRENTISS stole a swift glance at her watch, and stifled her amusement as she realised the gesture was being surreptitiously copied all around the classroom. Not that she could really blame the children, she thought tolerantly. The autumn term was the longest, and this half-term break was more than welcome—to the teachers as well as the pupils. When they came back after their week's holiday, everything would slide with ever-increasing momentum towards the hectic excitement of Christmas, and its attendant Nativity plays, carol concerts and frantic present-making.

A lot of her fellow staff members groaned both inwardly and aloud at the prospect, but Janna always found herself rather looking forward to Christmas, in spite of all the extra work. She enjoyed the yards of paper chains and the parties, and helping to cut out robins and holly which actually bore some resemblance to the real thing for the home-made calendars and cards.

It was this part of the year that she found so disturbing. She glanced out through the big window to the tree which dominated the centre of the tarmac playground. The summer had been long and lingering, but now, in late October, a wind with all the chill of winter in its breath was shaking loose the last remaining leaves and sending them drifting in little eddies to the ground.

The lunch bell was due to go at any moment. Quietly, she told the child at the top of each table to collect up the books and hand them in. There wouldn't be any work that afternoon. Mrs Parsons, the headmistress, had hired some films, and the children were seething with excitement, vehemently arguing the merits of Tom and Jerry over Bugs

Bunny. She chivvied them into a certain amount of quiet and order, and along the corridor to the school hall for lunch. It was mince, she noted wryly, with the soya bean which seemed an inevitable addition these days, and it was a taste she hadn't been able to acquire to far, although the children seemed to like it well enough. She wandered back towards the staffroom. She wasn't particularly hungry. She had an apple in her briefcase, and she would make do with that.

As she walked past the school office, Vivien Lennard, the school secretary, peered round the door at her. 'Oh, there you are, Janna. I was just going to send a kid with a note to find you. Colin rang to say he would pick you up in five minutes.'

'Oh.' Janna paused for a moment, taken aback. She did occasionally have lunch with Colin, but he usually gave her a fair amount of warning. She knew that if she'd spoken to Colin herself, she would have made an excuse. She didn't feel like indulging in a large and probably stodgy meal at the White Hart, whose dining room was Carrisford's only restaurant.

'Cheer up!' Vivien sounded amused. 'Anyone would think you'd just had the death sentence pronounced! Well, that comes later, dear—at the wedding. For now, you're just engaged to the lad, so why not enjoy it?'

Janna smiled in spite of herself, knowing quite well that Vivien herself was as happily married as it was almost possible to be.

'Sorry if I'm ruining your image of love's young dream,' she returned. 'I'm just feeling a little jaded, that's all. It's been damned hard work this term so far. This class hasn't been as easy to get to know as some that I've had.'

'Never mind.' Vivien gave her a pat on the arm. 'When you and Colin get married, all this will just seem like some horrible dream. He does still want you to give up work straight away, doesn't he?'

'Yes,' Janna agreed with something of an effort, 'he does.'

Vivien stared at her. 'Don't tell me you're having second thoughts!'

Janna smiled faintly. 'Oh, not about Colin. Just about giving up work. It seems so—so odd, somehow. I just can't visualise myself as a lady of leisure.'

'A lady of leisure—with Colin's home to run, and all that entertaining you'll be called on to do, not to mention having a family of your own some day? You're kidding!'

'I suppose it does sound ridiculous. But when I started my training I thought I'd be teaching for years to come.'

'The dedicated spinster, I suppose, with Prime Ministers coming to wring your gnarled hand and swear they got their inspiration from you.' Vivien's laugh was infectious. She gave Janna a shrewd all-encompassing glance from the sleek cap of smooth dark hair which curved forward on to her cheeks, and the slightly tilting green eyes, down over her slender but rounded figure to her slim legs and small feet in fashionably high-heeled shoes. 'I'm sorry, my dear, but you don't fit the image at all.'

In all but one thing, it suddenly occurred to her after she had gone back into her office and resumed her task of filling in the endless forms that were part of her daily routine. Janna was a lovely thing and had never lacked for masculine admirers, long before Colin Travers had arrived on the scene. Yet there had always been something cool, even remote about her, although Vivien had always considered her husband Bill was exaggerating when he described Janna as 'an icicle'. Nevertheless, there was a promise of generosity in the curves of Janna's mouth that Vivien could swear had never been fulfilled, and allied to this was the constant suggestion that Janna was holding herself back in some way—constantly reserved.

'One thing's certain,' Vivien told herself as she thrust an envelope into her typewriter and began to type the address. 'If she ever does let herself go, someone will be counting his blessings for the rest of his life.'

Meanwhile, the unconscious object of all this speculation

had retrieved her full-length suede coat from the cloakroom, and was standing near the main entrance watching out for Colin's car.

A group of older children, who would be attending the second dinner sitting, came racing over to her. 'Miss—Miss —have you seen that car?'

Alison Wade, who had been in her class the previous year, caught her hand. 'Come and see it, Miss. It's—it's fantastic!'

'It must be,' Janna said amusedly, knowing that Alison was not easily impressed.

Half-resignedly, she allowed herself to be shepherded round to the side of the building where the staff and visitors parked their cars, and her jaw dropped a little. Alison had not been exaggerating. She knew very little about cars and she could place neither the model nor its country of origin. What she could recognise was the understated suggestion of power and performance in the streamlined, low-slung shape, and an unmistakable aura of luxury.

The children were staring at it and murmuring, resisting the temptation to touch it and leave fingermarks on the immaculate pale grey body.

Kevin Daniel nudged her. 'Eh, Miss,' he said in awe, 'it's like something out of a James Bond film.' He pointed at the headlamps. 'D'you think there's concealed machine-guns there?'

'I doubt it,' Janna told him apologetically, but even she was taken aback by the instrument panel on the dashboard. Maybe there were no machine-guns, but she was sure every gadget in the history of the world was included somewhere in that terrifying array of dials and switches.

A car horn blared sharply, and involuntarily she stepped back, wondering just for a second if the car owner was somehow able to warn people away by some form of remote control ... Then she saw Colin's car parked outside the school gates, and chided herself for her own fancifulness. She paused long enough to shoo the children safely back to the playground and out of temptation's way, then went out of the gates where Colin was waiting impatiently, holding the passenger door open for her.

'We haven't got much time,' he remarked as he swung himself into the driving seat, leaning across and brushing his lips against her cheek.

Janna glanced at her watch. 'We've over an hour. The service at the White Hart isn't that slow and ...'

He shook his head. 'We aren't going there. There's something I want to show you first. We might manage a drink and a sandwich at the Crown afterwards.'

'The Crown?' Janna stared at him, puzzled. 'But that's out of town.'

He sent her a brief, triumphant smile. 'I know. Sit back, my sweet, and prepare for a surprise.'

Janna complied, faintly bewildered by the air of barely suppressed excitement that hung about Colin. He was generally so imperturbable, so much in control of his emotions. It was one of the things that she admired about him, and certainly an aspect of his character which explained his success in business. It was an open secret locally that Colin was the driving force now at Travers Engineering, and that his father, who had founded the firm, was content to be a figurehead, and leave the running of the company in Colin's hands.

Travers was the only large works in the locality, and it had expanded dramatically in recent years in spite of the generally depressed economic climate. With the expansion had come a change of role for Carrisford, with a brand new housing estate springing up on its outskirts, and a hurried building programme to add to the capacity of its primary and comprehensive schools. Yet in many ways it still remained a rather sleepy little market town, Janna thought with affection as Colin's car threaded its way through the crowded square bordered by tall grey stone buildings. The tradition was there in the market cross, and the square

Georgian town hall set firmly at one end of the market place.

It had always looked the same for as long as she could remember. She had gone away to do her training, and in many ways had been glad to go, and she still wasn't sure what had brought her back as a newly fledged teacher in her probationary year. Her parents were undemonstratively glad to see her. They regarded it as part of the scheme of things that the daughter of their marriage should live at home until she set out on a married life of her own. There was a reassuring sense of permanence, of stability about things, and Colin's advent into her life seemed, as far as her mother was concerned certainly, merely an inevitable piece in the pattern.

Janna and Colin had met two years earlier, when Colin had first come to the Carrisford works. Up to that time, he had merely been a name to many of the local people, having followed school and university with a prolonged training period, both abroad and at the other works in the north-west of England.

They had met at the cricket club one warm Saturday afternoon when Janna was helping some of the players' wives with the teas. When the match was ended prematurely by a drenching thunderstorm he had asked her to go out to dinner with him. Before many weeks had passed Janna knew she was being courted. At first, she could only feel dismay, but she soon discovered Colin had no intention of rushing her either physically or mentally into a relationship she was not prepared for. His pursuit of her, though determined, was leisurely. As she had come to know him better, she realised that this was not solely out of consideration for her, but because there was an instinctive element of caution in his nature. He too wanted to be absolutely sure before committing himself.

They had been officially engaged for just over three months now, and Janna had begun to sense a slight change in his attitude of late. They had not planned an exact date for their marriage, but she knew he was thinking in terms of the following spring. But though this had led to a new sense of urgency in their relationship, Janna had not discovered any determination in Colin to take it to a more intimate level which she might have expected. After all, he was going to be her husband. She wore his very expensive ring and was a frequent guest at his father's rather ostentatious house in the neighbouring dale. In many ways, there was not the slightest reason why they should hold back any longer. And yet ... Janna gripped her hands together in her lap until the brilliant solitaire she wore on her left hand bit into her flesh. At the back of her mind there was always that memory, no matter how deeply buried she thought it was. Savagely, she dammed it back into the recesses of her brain. It was over—had been over for years. Anyway, she'd been hardly more than a child. She couldn't still go on blaming herself for that ...

She dragged herself back into the present with a start, aware suddenly that the car had turned left at the last fork and was climbing steadily.

'The Crown's the other way.' She twisted around in her seat and looked at the grey town lying in the sheltered valley behind them. 'Darling, I know I said I had an hour, but it doesn't last for ever.'

'I know. But I do have a surprise for you, my love. Be patient.'

'All right.' She looked ahead of them uncertainly. 'But there's nothing up here, you know. Only Carrisbeck House.'

She was glad that Colin had no idea what an effort it cost her to say that.

'Correct. Clever girl! Go to the top of the class.'

To her dismay, the car was slowing, and Colin was indicating his intention to turn left.

'But we can't go in there,' she protested, fighting her panic. 'It—it's empty. It has been for years.'

'I know,' Colin said casually as they drove through the

gates and up the long curve of the drive. 'Tragedy, isn't it?'

Towering rhododendrons crowded on each side of the gravel. The last time she had driven up this drive they had been covered in blossom, she thought confusedly, and she had sat in the back of a much less opulent car than Colin's, almost sick with excitement because she was going to a party at Carrisbeck House and because *he* would be there. And because tonight—that night—she was going to make him notice her.

She shivered suddenly, closing her eyes.

'Grey goose flying over your grave?' Colin's voice was almost jocular. The car had stopped and when she opened her eyes, it wasn't a nightmare. It was really happening. They were really parked in front of Carrisbeck House. It looked just the same, with the short flight of shallow steps leading up to the front door. The only difference was that the two great stone urns which flanked the steps looked empty and neglected. Mrs Tempest had always kept them filled with flowers, she thought. Summer or winter, it seemed there had always been something in bloom to welcome you at the door. Now there was nothing, and the curtainless windows seemed to stare down at her inimically as if they were remembering that other Janna Prentiss, not quite seventeen and much more sure of herself than she had ever been since.

'We can't go in.' Her voice sounded strained and breathless even in her own ears. 'I know it's empty, but it still belongs to Colonel Tempest even so . . .'

Colin reached into his pocket and produced a bunch of keys tied to a label.

'No longer, I'm afraid. I'm surprised you haven't heard, but it will be in the *Advertiser* at the weekend. Colonel Tempest died last week, so the house is on the market. Barry Windrush's father is handling the sale and Barry gave me a tip-off.' He gave a swift, excited laugh and drew her unresponsive body against his. 'Don't you understand, darling? That's going to be our house!'

The silence was endless and then she said stupidly, 'But—we can't buy that.'

'What's to prevent us? Don't be an idiot, my sweet.' The affection in his voice had an added note of exasperation. 'I've spoken to Dad, and he's given us the go-ahead. In fact, he's all for it. It's ideal—close to the works, big enough to do all the entertaining, but not so massive that you'd need an immense staff to help you run it. I believe the Tempests had a housekeeper. She's been keeping an eye on the place, I understand, so its condition should be quite reasonable. And her husband has been keeping the garden in order. I know they're neither of them young any more, but Barry reckons they might be quite willing to stay on, if they were asked, and that would solve all sorts of problems. Janna, what is it? Are you all right?'

'Yes, I'm fine,' she lied, trying desperately to catch at the rags of her self-control. She gave him a meaningless smile. 'But you can't be serious, Colin. How can we live here? It's the old *Tempest* house. Everyone knows that.'

He shrugged irritably. 'No doubt, but what happens now that there are no more "old Tempests" to occupy it? Do you really think a lovely place like this should be left to moulder away and fall down? Not if I know it. Come on, darling,' he added with an impatient look at his watch. 'It's you that has to get back. Come and have a look round.'

She had no option but to obey. If she refused to go in at all, he would have every reason to accuse her of being illogical, and she couldn't explain.

As they reached the top of the steps, she said carefully. 'But there are more Tempests, aren't there? What about the—the nephew?'

Colin shrugged, intent on fitting the key into the lock. 'I wouldn't know, darling. I didn't even know there was a nephew. Whatever has happened to him, he hasn't inherited the estate.'

The big panelled hall was just as she remembered it, with the sweep of the stairs leading up to the galleried landing above.

'Barry says they used to hold dances in here.' Colin looked around. 'I must say there's room enough. I'm quite sorry I never came to any of them. I suppose you never did, darling? You were probably too young.'

'I came—once,' she said, then walked over to the drawing room door and turned the handle. It was a beautiful room. She had always loved it with the great French windows looking out over the sloping gardens, and the gleam of the river in the distance. It looked forlorn without the deep sofas and chairs with their charming chintz covers. She could see the marks on the walls where pictures had once hung. The fire-irons still stood in the hearth to the left of the empty grate where sweet-smelling pine cones and logs had once burned. There had been a low-seated Victorian chair by that hearth once, she remembered, and Janna the school-girl had once sat nervously on its edge, clutching a bone china plate while Mrs Tempest poured tea and asked what she intended to do when she left school. And she had said quickly, 'I'd like to travel,' and tried to stop herself glancing too eagerly towards the door, waiting for the moment when it would open and *he* would come in. Rian. Rian Tempest, Colonel Tempest's nephew and sole relative, who worked as a foreign correspondent on a newspaper and travelled all over the world.

But he did not come, and Janna's excuse for her visit— she had volunteered to deliver the parish magazine for Mrs Hardwick who had a sprained ankle—was a complete waste. And she still had dozens of the beastly things to hike around in the sun. It was less a sense of duty and more a fear of retribution, divine or all too human, which had stopped her giving them decent burial behind some convenient hedge. But perhaps, she'd thought, giving her imagination full rein, Mrs Tempest might mention that evening over dinner that she'd been there. 'That lovely Prentiss child'—which wasn't really conceit because she'd heard it said so many times, and Rian might take a new look at her and see that she wasn't really a child any more but a woman—a woman ...

As she stood in the middle of the empty drawing room, Janna's cheeks burned at the memory of her own naïveté. It had all seemed so simple then. You stretched out your hand and said 'Give me' and a kindly Providence dispensed whatever was required, because you were lovely and so nearly seventeen and spoiled by everyone.

Someone had left a key on the inside of the french windows leading to the terrace. The key was stiff in the lock, but eventually it yielded and Janna walked outside into the fresh air. Somewhere at the back of her mind a warning voice was shouting at her, 'Don't look back.' All these years it had worked so well. Glimpsing the house as she drove past on her way somewhere else, hearing the Tempests mentioned, she had managed to avert her gaze and closed her ears.

It had been difficult, though, when she had heard that Mrs Tempest had died. She had never been a robust woman, Janna thought, remembering the finely boned face under its coronet of silvering hair. Colonel Tempest had always been openly protective towards his wife, and Rian's attitude to his aunt had echoed this.

But there had been no sign of weakness about Mrs Tempest that night. She had driven Janna home, her back straight as a ramrod, her gaze fixed unerringly on the road ahead. At her gate, she had said, 'You are quite well, Janna? Then I will bid you goodnight.' She had driven away and Janna had never seen or heard from her again. It had only been a few weeks later that the house had been shut up, and the Colonel and his wife had moved away. There was speculation, naturally, but it did not take the form that Janna had feared. It was taken for granted that Mrs Tempest's health would not stand up to another northern winter. Someone in the post office had even remarked that she'd 'been showing her age lately, poor lady'.

No one, luckily, had linked Rian's abrupt departure several weeks before with the Colonel's decision to close the house and move. Rian was a law unto himself. He came and went when and where his job took him. Everyone knew the Colonel had been disappointed because his nephew hadn't followed him into the Army, but it was accepted that Rian had a mind of his own, and no one could say the Colonel wasn't proud of the way the boy had turned out. More like a son than a nephew, people said, and that was the way it should be as Rian had no parents of his own any more.

A much younger Janna had always been among the crowd of worshippers when Rian, who played cricket for his university, turned out for the local club during the summer vacation. She had begged his autograph once on the corner of a score card and treasured it until it literally fell to pieces.

There had been a quality about him even then which had set him apart from the rest, although she had been too young to analyse it. His movements were unstud'edly elegant and economical, and although he certainly wasn't good-looking in the film or television star mould, there was a latent attraction in his dark, saturnine features. When he smiled, his charm was magical, almost wicked. It hinted that its owner was not disposed to take anything really seriously, especially you, no matter how delightful he might find you, and it was irresistible. Or Janna had found it so.

She stepped forward to the edge of the terrace, wrapping her arms tightly across her body. The wind was blowing straight off the Pennines, and its force had an added bite.

'Darling, what on earth are you doing out here? It's freezing.' Colin's voice sounded rather plaintive as he made his way out through the french windows to join her.

'Blowing the cobwebs away,' she said, and heaven knew it was the truth. But would it work?

Colin, to her relief, took the remark at its face value.

'The place could do with an airing,' he remarked. 'But

I can't smell any damp, can you? It all seems in pretty good
nick. Shall we have a look upstairs?'

'You go ahead,' she said. 'I'll join you in a minute. I
want to enjoy this view for a while. It's a long time since
I've seen it.'

A long time—seven years, to be exact. Seven years since
she had come out of that antique auction further up the
dale with her father and found herself face to face with
Rian, come to collect his aunt who had been bidding for
some china figures. For a moment she had barely recognised him. He had always been thin, but now his face was
harder and older, the dark eyes under their lazily drooping
lids suddenly wary. He had answered her father's jovial
greeting with a smile and a handshake, and then had turned
to her, his smile widening.

'Of course I remember Janna,' he responded to her
father's query. 'I'm waiting impatiently for her to grow up.'

It was the teasing, slightly flirtatious remark that he
might have made to the schoolgirl daughter of any old
acquaintance. She could see it now. Why couldn't she have
seen it then?

Because I didn't want to, she thought, gripping the terrace balustrade with suddenly shaking hands. Because in
that brief instant, on the heels of his joking remark, she had
found a focus for all those barely understood adolescent
yearnings. Still half a child, every demand of her awaken-
ing womanhood had become crystallised in Rian. And her
egotism, burnished by the knowledge of her legion of
admirers in the local Sixth Form and the Young Farmers'
club, had done the rest.

She wanted Rian, so it must follow as the night did the
day that he wanted her.

Janna winced, recalling how simple it had all seemed
then. It had not taken her long to find out why Rian was in
Carrisford. He was on an extended sick leave recovering
after a fever contracted in a jungle war, but the fact that he
was officially convalescent did not prevent him throwing

himself into the social life of the district.

Just how fully Janna only realised at breakfast one morning, when her father casually remarked to her mother, 'I see young Tempest has taken up with Barbara Kenton. Bit of a lass, isn't she?'

'You could say that,' her mother had replied with a repressive glance in Janna's direction.

Janna had pushed away her cereal bowl with a sudden sick feeling. She knew all about Barbara Kenton. Within the limitations of the area, Barbara was fairly notorious. In her last years at school, there had always been jokes about her, and comments scribbled on walls. Then, she had been a tall, sleepy-eyed blonde whose clothes always seemed just too skimpy for her voluptuous body. Now she was working as a receptionist in the White Hart, and making little attempt to conceal her overt sexuality.

Her father was speaking again. 'Well, you can't blame the lad. Plenty of time before he needs to think of settling down. But I bet he hasn't told his uncle. Bit of a Puritan, the old Colonel, if you ask me.'

Janna got up from the table, feeling her cheeks beginning to burn angrily. Collecting her school bag from the hall, she told herself vehemently that Rian couldn't like Barbara Kenton. He just couldn't! She was so vile and obvious. But that evening at the Midsummer barbecue she was given plenty of evidence to the contrary. Rian was there, and Barbara was with him, clinging to his arm at every opportunity. They left the barbecue early, and Janna overheard a few of the ribald remarks when their departure was observed. It was her first real experience of jealousy, and it was cruel and hurtful. The evening was ruined for her, and as she lay in bed that night, tossing restlessly in a vain attempt to capture some sleep, images of Rian with Barbara kept superimposing themselves on her mind.

It wasn't a great consolation to find that Barbara could not consider him her exclusive property either. She was just one of a long list of girls that Rian escorted to dances and

parties, and drove to dinner in his sports car as June lengthened into July. But Janna, to her chagrin, was not.

They met everywhere, of course, and he always spoke
pleasantly to her, but at the same time he made no attempt
to further their acquaintance. To her dismay, she realised
that he was treating her as he would any other of the youngsters. She did everything she could to get him to notice her,
abandoning her own crowd of friends and hanging about
on the fringes of his, flirting outrageously with anyone who
gave her any encouragement, and dancing without a trace
of inhibition with any partners who offered themselves.
Rian did not offer. Occasionally she caught him watching
her, an expression of faint amusement in his dark eyes, but
he always held maddeningly aloof.

But at last her chance came. There was a Young Farmers'
buffet dance, and Janna managed to wangle herself an invitation from Philip Avery, who was only a couple of years
Rian's junior. Her parents did not approve, she knew, but
they could not forbid her to go without offending the
Averys. Besides, Philip was eminently respectable, and his
eight years' seniority to Janna was the only real complaint
they could make against him.

Extreme behaviour had got her nowhere, she decided, so
she would see what the utmost circumspection would
achieve. At first it did not seem to be achieving very much
at all. Rian's eyebrows had risen when Philip had arrived
at his table with his partner, and his greeting to Janna was
cool. Everyone else in the party was at least five years older
than she was, and Janna soon began to feel very out of
things. Much of the general conversation was lost on her
as she did not know the people or the incidents being re-
ferred to. Philip was good-natured enough, but it was
obvious from his attitude that he now rather regretted bringing her, and Janna guessed that he had been teased by some
of his contemporaries for cradle-snatching. Suppressed tears
of mortification made her eyes sparkle even more brilliantly
than usual, and she held her head high as she sipped her

fruit juice, and tried to pretend that it didn't matter that she was the only person at the table not old enough to order something alcoholic.

It was just after the interval that the miracle happened. She came back from the cloakroom to find everyone else dancing and Rian sitting alone at the table. He rose courteously as she approached and held the chair as she sat down, but she knew that he was hiding his annoyance at the situation. Inwardly she was jubilant.

She smiled at him, using her lowered eyelashes quite shamelessly.

'Aren't you going to ask me to dance?'

'I wasn't,' he said dampeningly. 'However, if you insist.' He rose and held out his hand.

She swallowed down a swift feeling of humiliation, and accompanied him on to the dance floor. It was a fast-moving beat number, and there was no opportunity for conversation. She could have cried with disappointment. She knew she could make him interested in her, if only—only she was given the chance. Like an answer to her prayer, the lights dimmed and the band's tempo changed to a slow smoochy number. Amid wolf whistles and catcalls, couples went willingly into each other's arms. Janna glanced shyly at Rian and saw that amusement was battling with exasperation on his face. For one appalled moment, she thought he was going to take her back to the table in front of everyone. Then, with a slight shrug, he held out his arms.

For a few seconds she was too unnerved with happiness to be aware of anything other than she was at last in his arms where she had wanted to be. Then her senses began to report other messages, the sheer hard muscularity of his body against hers, the sharp, expensive smell of the cologne he used, and almost involuntarily she moved closer to him, pressing herself invitingly against him and sliding her arms round his waist under his jacket.

For a moment he tensed, and she heard him give a soft, unamused laugh.

'You, my sweet Janna, have all the makings of a first-class witch—but of course you know that,' he murmured.

'I don't know anything except that this is the first time I've ever danced with you.' She tipped her head back and looked up at him, deliberately provocative.

He tapped the end of her nose with a careless finger. 'Don't try your tricks on me, little one. I've seen them all before and performed by experts. Go and cut your milk teeth on someone your own age, and I don't mean Philip Avery.'

When she spoke, her voice shook with anger. 'Don't be so—so bloody patronising! You're only ten years older than me, Rian Tempest, so what gives you the right to criticise my conduct?'

He grinned down into her furious face. 'That's more like it, Janna. The sophisticated siren bit doesn't suit you, you know. You've got years ahead of you for that. I preferred the kid with ice-cream round her mouth who used to tail after me at cricket matches.'

'How very sad,' she said, struggling to regain her poise. 'I'm afraid I buried her some time ago, along with my ankle socks and the braces on my teeth.'

'It's sadder than you know,' he answered briefly. There was a long pause, then he said quite gently, 'Look, Janna, I know—or rather I suspect—what you're up to. I won't pretend I'm not flattered. I wouldn't be human if I wasn't. You're young, very lovely, and very desirable. It's a combination that adds up to dynamite and I—I don't want to be around when the explosion happens. I have enough excitement in my work. When I'm on leave, I'm looking for some rest and relaxation.'

'Is that what you get from Barbara Kenton?' some inner demon made her ask.

His eyes narrowed dangerously. 'I hardly think that's any of your business,' he drawled. 'But let me advise you against trying to emulate her example. You—er—lack the basic equipment at the moment.' He let his eyes rest insolently on the modest cleavage revealed by the dipping neckline of her pale yellow dress.

Her cheeks were flaming. 'You—you swine!' she breathed.

He bowed his head in ironic acknowledgment. 'That's a safer thing to be in your eyes than the answer to the maiden's prayer, Janna,' he said drily. 'Now shall we sit the rest of this out?'

She had wept bitterly that night, but had risen the following morning with all the mercurial optimism of youth. He had said she was lovely and desirable, as well as being young. She would build on that.

She came back to the present with a start as Colin said irritably, 'Are you going to spend all day gazing at this damned view?'

She turned. He was standing in the open french windows, staring at her reproachfully. 'It's nearly time for you to get back, and you haven't even looked at the bedrooms or the kitchens.'

She looked down at the stone flags. 'I don't think I can live here, Colin,' she said at last.

'What?' His voice rose incredulously.

'We—we don't have to buy this house, do we?' She moistened her lips and stared desperately around her. 'It's too big, for one thing. There must be seven or eight bedrooms at least. You said yourself that we'd need staff. I'd rather looked forward to coping by myself—when we were first married, at least.'

Colin's frown deepened. 'I don't know what's got into you, Janna. I thought you knew that you weren't going to be Little Mrs Average in her three-bedroomed semi. That isn't our sort of life, darling. You must be realistic about it.'

She bit her lip. 'I'm sorry, Colin. I—I just don't care for this house. I can't visualise myself ever living here.'

His expression became slightly more indulgent. 'I've rushed you a bit, haven't I, darling? I'm sorry, it was stupid of me. I just thought you'd be as thrilled as I am about it all.' He walked over to her and slid his arms round her waist, pressing his lips to the side of her neck. 'Forgive me?' he whispered.

'Of course.' The smile was difficult, but she made the effort.

He was silent for a minute or two. Then, 'It is a glorious view,' he beguiled her. 'Are you quite sure you want to let it go?' He waited, but she made no reply. 'Think about it, Janna,' he said persuasively. 'Properties like this don't come on the market any old day, you know.' He kissed her again. 'And you're so lovely,' he muttered thickly. 'It's just the setting you need. You were born to be the mistress of this house, darling.'

Suddenly she wanted to be free of his seeking hands. Nervously, she pulled away, trying to laugh. 'Colin, I've got to get back to school. I'm sorry I've disappointed you, and I will think it over, I promise.'

'I can't ask more than that.' He linked his fingers companionably through hers and led her back into the drawing room, locking the french windows behind them. 'I know you'll change your mind, my sweet. I'll arrange for a survey to be done, and we'll come again next week when we have more time and go all over the place.'

'Yes,' she said quietly, 'we'll do that, if you wish.'

Conversation was desultory as they drove back through Carrisford, and parked outside the school gates. Colin took her hand. 'Dinner tonight?'

She hesitated. 'I don't think so. I ought to wash my hair.'

'It looks fine to me,' he said. 'But you know best. I'll ring you tomorrow.' He lifted her hand to his lips.

She stood on the pavement and watched the car drive away, feeling as if her entire world had been turned upside down. The safe walls of security and convention that she had built so painstakingly up around herself over the past few years showed every sign of tumbling around her, and it was an uncomfortable feeling at the least.

Colin was right, of course, she thought miserably. The

house had everything to recommend it. If it had been any other house anywhere in the locality she would have shared his enthusiasm. She had always known that it would be part of her duties as his wife to entertain his guests and have foreign buyers to stay, and she had looked forward to it.

But the house—that house—did not belong to them and never could, no matter how much money Colin's father might put up. It was the Tempest house, and it belonged by rights to Rian Tempest, and it was her fault and hers alone that Rian had not inherited it. Her fault that it had stood empty for all these years. No one had ever accused her, but she knew it just the same, knew that Rian had left his uncle's house seven years before in bitterness and disgrace because of her, and that the Colonel had died without forgiving him.

And the fact that the knowledge of her guilt was confined to her and only one other person in the world now did not ease her conscience in the slightest.

Faintly in the distance, she could hear the bell for afternoon school begin to ring, and she turned and began to walk up the drive. Over in the playground, the children were being lined up by the teacher on duty, and Janna turned slightly to watch, not noticing where she was going.

She did not hear the sound of the car's engine. The first warning of its presence was the blare of the horn, and she stepped hurriedly out of its way, flattening herself against an adjacent wall with a word of apology on her lips. She glanced at the driver's seat, wondering incuriously who the owner of such an exotic vehicle might be and what business brought him to a small country school in the middle of the day. She couldn't think of any of the parents whose finances would run to a supercharged machine like that. The half-smile died on her lips. For one incredulous moment, she thought she must be dreaming, that it must be an image created by her overcharged emotional state.

The car braked softly beside her, and the driver's window rolled noiselessly downwards, at the press of a button, she thought hysterically, digging her nails into the palms of her hands. A pair of dark eyes met hers expressionlessly, then moved slowly and consideringly downwards, lingering on her white face, and the trembling limbs she could neither control nor dissemble.

'Hello, Janna,' said Rian Tempest.

Then the car accelerated forward, with a low, fierce growl like some huge menacing beast, and he was gone.

CHAPTER TWO

JANNA shut her bedroom door and sank down on the bed with a heartfelt sigh of relief. Her head was throbbing painfully, and her confused state of emotion, coupled with apprehension, had made her feel physically sick.

She did not know how she had managed to get through the afternoon with a semblance of normality. She had sat in the darkened hall with her class, watching the film show with unseeing eyes, laughing obediently when everyone else did at the technicoloured cavortings without the slightest realisation of what was going on. Luckily the Walt Disney adventure and the cartoons which preceded it had occupied everyone else's attention, so Janna's wan appearance and tightly gripped hands passed unnoticed.

Her mother, however, was not so easily to be put off. She had watched with puckered brows while Janna pushed her evening meal, uneaten, round her plate, but had accepted her halting explanation that she thought she might be starting a migraine. Mrs Prentiss had been a migraine sufferer all her life and was always eagle-eyed to detect incipient signs of it in anyone close to her. She had tutted distressedly over Janna, pressed some painkillers on her, and recommended that she lie down in her darkened room. Janna was thankful to accept the medicine and the advice.

Now that she was alone, at least she did not have to pretend any more. She turned and lay full-length on her stomach across the bed, pillowing her chin on her folded arms.

Rian Tempest was back in Carrisford. After all these years without a sign, a word even, he had returned, and now her peace of mind had gone for ever.

She closed her eyes, trying to erase from her mind the

26

memory of that long look he had given her before he had driven off. It had emphasised more clearly than words could do that he had not forgotten anything which had passed between them seven years before. Not forgotten—and not forgiven either. But what else did she expect? What she had done to Rian was unforgivable. She had always known that.

She shivered, pressing her body further into the yielding softness of the eiderdown as if she was seeking some kind of sanctuary. When she had been a child, and there had been some small disaster to be faced, it had always been a comfort to drag the bedclothes round her—even over her head—and tell herself that no one would ever find her now.

Yet Rian had found her, she thought, as she had always feared that he would even with the false sense of security the passing years had given her.

But why had he come back? she asked herself almost despairingly. Now that his aunt and uncle were both dead and he must know for certain that the house and estate were not his, what was there to draw him back to Carrisford? The possibilities that suggested themselves were too disturbing to contemplate.

She turned restlessly on to her side, wishing for the first time in her life that she had a sleeping tablet. Something that would blot out thinking and reasoning—and above all remembering for a few hours. The adult equivalent of drawing the bedclothes over one's head, she told herself wryly.

What did he intend? she asked herself, but no immediate answer was forthcoming. Rian had always been totally unpredictable, she thought. That was why she had continued to pursue him, confident that he was not as impervious to her as he had tried to maintain. She had the memory of his reaction to her while she had been in his arms to buoy up her hopes as well. He might have spoken of his own indifference, but his body had betrayed him with its instinctive response to her proximity. And there was an element of

challenge in the affair now. She would make him admit
that he wanted her, in deed as well as word. She would
make him grovel.

Janna gave a groan and buried her face in her hands.
Why, oh, why had she been so sure she could do so, when
all the evidence suggested the contrary? God knew she had
received fair warning, so she could blame no one for what
had happened subsequently but herself.

She had seen little of Rian in the week following the
dance, do what she might. It had been during this time that
she had paid her abortive visit to Carrisbeck House with the
parish magazines, she recalled with a pang. But he seemed
to be avoiding his usual haunts, or at least avoiding her
while she was there, and she had to be content with a couple
of unsatisfactory glimpses of him driving his car, once with
Barbara Kenton's blonde head conspicuously close to his
dark one.

Her obsession was beginning to be noticed by her friends,
and a few sly hints were dropped, which she ignored in
spite of the feelings raging inside her. Geoff Christie, whom
she had been dating in a desultory manner before Rian's
return, soon became peeved at her indifference and began
taking out one of her friends. From being the centre of
attention, Janna began to find that she was now becoming
an outsider among her contemporaries, but she told herself
defiantly that she did not care. If she was lonely, then she
had chosen to be so, and anyway nothing mattered except
Rian.

Her schoolwork began to suffer, and she found herself
the target for tart remarks from her teachers, who could
not understand why such a previously bright and interested
girl had suddenly become such an introspective dreamer.
She could not sleep either. Many nights she lay awake for
hours, tormented by feelings that she could only dimly
comprehend. It was a warm summer, so she was able to
blame the heat for her sleeplessness and shadowed eyes.
There were even nights when she let herself quietly out of

the sleeping house and walked through the silent streets,
through the town and up into the hills, encountering nothing more than a few startled sheep. Except once.

Janna rolled on to her back and stared up at the ceiling
as she remembered that particular night. As it happened,
she had not been for one of her solitary walks. She had
been visiting a girl friend whose parents owned a farm a few
miles up the dale from Carrisford, and she was cycling
back rather later than she had intended. She was not worried about it. Her parents would probably think she was
spending the night at Marion's as she had done in the past,
she reassured herself.

She came across the Carrisbeck bridge and slowed for the
bend, when she noticed a car pulled off the road and into
the shelter of the trees which crowded to the edge of the
highway. She recognised it instantly, even though its lights
were off, and checked.

Her first thought was that Rian might be in the wood
with Barbara, and she had to suppress a pang of jealous
anger, but reason prevailed, pointing out that this particular clump of trees was hardly an appropriate place for a
lovers' tryst. It was far too near the river for one thing, and
invariably damp. So what was he up to? she wondered.
She got off her bike and wheeled it to the side of the road,
depositing it near Rian's car, then set off down the narrow
muddy track which was all that constituted a path. There
was no sound of voices, however hushed, just the distant
murmur of the river and closer at hand the heart-thudding
cry of an owl just above her head.

Janna expelled her breath in a slow sigh of sheer fright,
then went cautiously on.

She paused as she emerged from the trees where the
ground fell away sharply to the river bank below, and a
mischievous smile curved her lips. The river at this point
was wide, and the current deep and sluggish. It was one
of the places recognised locally as being safe for bathing,
and Rian, she saw, was taking full advantage of the fact.

Against the silvery sheen of the water, his hair looked black and gleaming, and she could see the long lithe turn of his body as he moved easily through the water.

She slithered down on to the bank, found what she was looking for—his clothes in a neat pile—and sat on them demurely, waiting for him to notice her. But somewhat to her pique, he was obviously too absorbed in his own pleasure to notice he had company, and eventually she was obliged to draw his attention to the fact by clearing her throat noisily.

He dived under the water and came up a few feet from the bank, treading water, and shaking the drops from his face and hair.

'Janna,' he said resignedly. 'What the hell are you doing here?'

'You're not the only person who gets the urge to go moonlight bathing,' she said sweetly. 'Wouldn't you like some company?'

'No, I wouldn't,' he said with an air of restraint. 'Be a good girl and push off—please.'

She pouted, triumphantly aware that she had the whip hand for once. 'It's a free country,' she pointed out. 'And this is one of my favourite spots. Nor is it part of your uncle's estate. You can't make me go.'

'No, I can't,' he acknowledged. 'I hoped I wouldn't have to, and that asking you nicely might be enough.'

'Oh, but it isn't,' she said, and smiled. 'Now if you asked me nicely to stay—that might be different.'

'Indeed it might,' he said drily. 'And what's my next line? Come on in—the water's fine?'

'Thank you for the kind invitation,' she said, studiedly polite. 'But it may have escaped your attention that I haven't brought my swimsuit with me.'

'No.' He swam in a wide circle. 'Just as I'm sure it hasn't escaped your attention that I haven't brought mine either.'

Not for the world would she have admitted that it had not occurred to her.

'Oh, but that doesn't matter,' she said with assumed nonchalance, thankful that the darkness hid her warm cheeks. 'And—and I do know what a naked man looks like, you know.'

'In practice, or merely in theory?' The gleam of his smile mocked her. 'Janna Joins the Permissive Society, and other titles. I suppose it makes a change from the Pony Club.'

'Very amusing,' she said calmly. 'Have you heard the one about having the last laugh? It can't be getting any warmer in that water, and I happen to be sitting on your clothes. All of them.'

'Right on all counts,' he agreed reflectively. 'The situation is a little one-sided, I must admit.' He swam round again, this time coming right up to the bank. 'All right, Janna, I resign. Why not join me? It's a very warm night, and I promise to turn my back like a gentleman if that's what you're waiting for.'

She wasn't altogether certain what she was waiting for. She moistened her lips rather nervously. Dreams and imaginings were one thing; having them translated into quite such realistic terms as a moonlight bathing party for two in the nude, quite another.

'What's the matter, Janna?' She couldn't see the expression on Rian's face, but the taunt in his tone was unmistakable. 'Chicken?'

'Certainly not,' she said untruthfully. 'It—it just looks a bit cold, that's all.'

He laughed softly. 'I'll think of a way of keeping you warm, sweet witch.'

There had to be an answer to that, but Janna couldn't think of it for the life of her. Her mouth was suddenly dry, and she was trembling violently inside. One part of her wanted, childishly, to run, but another, more insidious voice was persuading her to remain.

When she spoke, her voice was higher than usual and oddly breathless.

'All right,' she said. She got up slowly, shivering a little although there was barely a hint of a breeze. The water rippled glossily as Rian swam one long, lazy stroke nearer. Her fingers, made suddenly clumsy, hesitated on the buttons of her shirt.

'You said you'd turn your back,' she reminded him lamely.

'If that's what you want.' There was a warm persuasive note in his voice, which made her gasp as if he had caressed her. 'Is it, lovely Janna?'

She had taken two unwary steps towards him before she realised the trap that had been set for her. Steely fingers, cold and wet, clamped round her ankle. Off balance already, she stumbled, and within a second she was flying through the air, or so it seemed, to land in the water in an undignified and painful belly-flop. She came back to the surface, winded and choking, having swallowed half the river in her astonishment.

On the bank, Rian was fastening the belt of his jeans and observing her flounderings with sardonic amusement.

'I don't think you'll ever make the Olympic squad,' he observed, judicially, pulling his dark sweater over his head. 'But the local life-saving team might be glad of a volunteer. I've heard they prefer them fully dressed.'

'You bastard!' she screamed at him.

'Such language from one so young,' he said reprovingly. 'If it's any consolation to you, I was tempted for a while, and I'm warning you, Janna, stay in your own league from now on.' He half turned to go. 'And I meant what I said about keeping you warm. I don't know how you got here, and I don't care much. I presume you cycled, or walked, so you can get home the same way—only faster. It's a balmy enough night. You shouldn't even catch cold.' He was gone.

Janna hauled herself out of the water and heard his car engine start up in the distance. Tears of rage and humiliation mingled with the drops of water on her face, as she stood dripping and bedraggled on the bank. She would never forgive him, she swore savagely to herself. And she would make him pay for this if it was the last thing she did.

She was walking round the market a few days later and had stopped to examine some remnants of material on a stall, when a hand descended on her arm and Rian's voice close to her ear said, 'None the worse for your ducking, I see.'

She wrenched herself forcibly free, and gave him a wrathful look.

'No thanks to you,' she said distinctly. 'I might have drowned—or gone down with pneumonia.'

'Hardly,' he said drily. 'I was sure somehow you'd manage to survive, Janna.'

'Thank you.' Her tone held bitterness. 'I know better than to regard that as a compliment.'

He sighed. 'Is that what you want—compliments?'

She stared down at her feet. 'You know what I want,' she muttered at last. 'I want you to treat me as if I was a woman.'

'Then stop behaving like a child,' he said, but his voice was gentler and held a trace of laughter. 'How old are you, Janna?'

'I shall be seventeen in just over two weeks' time.' She sent him a hostile look. 'I suppose to you I'm sixteen.'

'Stop supposing,' he said patiently. 'Come and have coffee with me instead.'

'Are you serious?' she asked incredulously.

'I think so.' There was an edge to his voice. 'It's only a hot drink I'm offering, not an invitation to bed.'

She flushed indignantly and he gave a slight groan. 'God help me, this was meant to be a peace move, not a resumption of hostilities. Come and have coffee, Janna.' His thumb moved caressingly on the soft flesh of her arm, sending a pleasant tingle through her senses. He grinned at her and she thought furiously that he probably knew quite well the effect that his casual touch was having on her.

He pulled her arm through his and led her off through the market-day crowds. The town's most popular café was situated in rooms at the rear of the baker's shop, and they lingered to make a selection of cream cakes at the counter before continuing to the rear and finding an unoccupied corner table.

'Well, this is pleasant.' Rian pushed the sugar bowl towards her.

She helped herself to a spoonful, her lips compressed.

'Please don't patronise me,' she said eventually.

'Nothing was further from my thoughts,' he returned mildly. 'Don't be so prickly, Janna.'

She stirred the spoon round the cup, watching the swirl of the liquid. 'Can you blame me?'

'Not altogether, perhaps, otherwise I shouldn't be here.' He reached his hand across the table and clasped hers lightly. 'Pax, sweet witch. I can't be your lover, but I could be your friend, if you'd let me.'

'On the grounds that half a loaf is better than no bread at all?' She gave him a defiant look. 'Is it really so impossible? Funnily enough, I got the distinct impression that you fancied me.'

'I plead guilty as charged,' he said slowly. He released her hand and sat back in his chair. 'Janna, you may well be counting the hours to your seventeenth birthday, but I was going through the same process ten years ago. There's no way around that.'

'Ten years isn't such a tremendous gap.'

'At this precise moment, it seems a lifetime.' He drank some of the coffee, grimaced slightly and pushed it aside. 'Apart from anything else, did no one ever tell you that sometimes the man prefers to make the running?'

She blushed vividly. 'I just wanted you to notice me,' she claimed in a low voice.

'As if anyone with normal faculties could possibly overlook you!' He gave her a wry look. 'You're a spectacular lass, Janna. If you were a few years older, you'd have to fight me off.'

'That's a great comfort,' she said past the lump in her

throat. 'I think I'd better go. Thanks for the coffee.'

'Oh, hell.' He pushed a hand through his dark hair. 'This is not turning out at all as I expected.'

'Does anything ever?' She picked up her leather shoulder bag and rose. She walked to the doorway through the clustering tables and disappeared, oblivious of the curious stares being cast in her direction from all over the room.

Janna climbed wearily off the bed and padded across the room to the window. She dragged the curtains shut with jerky movements, closing out the darkness.

She glanced restlessly around her. Her briefcase stood beside the desk in the corner. It contained her record book, among other things. She could check on her syllabus, plan her work for next half-term. Anything would be better than this constant retrospection, yet she doubted her ability to concentrate on anything more than her personal problems. Wherever she looked, Rian's face seemed to be imprinted on her vision, dark and vengeful.

She started as the sound of the doorbell pealed through the house, and for one crazy moment, panic filled her. Then common sense came to her rescue and she told herself that it might well be visitors for her parents. But a minute or two later there was a light tap on the door and Mrs Prentiss peeped in at her.

Her brows rose a little as she saw that Janna was neither undressed nor in bed.

'Vivien's downstairs, dear. I told her you might be asleep ...' Her voice tailed away questioningly, and Janna forced a smile.

'I feel much better, actually. I'll come down.'

Vivien was waiting in the sitting room. 'Poor old thing,' she exclaimed sympathetically as Janna entered. 'I didn't know you were a migraine sufferer. How rotten! Yet I thought you looked rather peaky when you dashed off after school.' She delved in her handbag and produced an envelope. 'That's why I'm here, really. What with you being out at lunch time, and then the films, Mrs Parsons didn't get a chance to have a word with you, so she's written you this note instead.'

'Note?' Janna took it, wrinkling her brow. 'This is all very official. What is it? The sack?'

'Hardly.' Vivien grinned at her. 'Of course, I was forgetting that you'd missed all the excitement at lunchtime. We're going to have a new pupil—a little girl—and Mrs P. is putting her in your class.'

'That's hardly my idea of excitement,' Janna said dryly. 'What is she? A second Einstein?'

Vivien shrugged. 'Who knows? Apparently she's part Vietnamese—on her mother's side. She has this enormously long name which means Flower of Morning—rather pretty, don't you think?—but her father calls her Fleur.'

Janna paused in the act of tearing open the envelope. Her eyes flew to Vivien's face with sudden, painful intensity. 'Her father—do you mean he is European?'

'And how,' Vivien said cheerfully. 'In fact you probably know him. Beth and Lorna do, anyway, and they were very impressed. Apparently his uncle used to live hereabouts some years ago. And even Bill's heard of the nephew —Rian Tempest. Says he's some kind of high-pressure journalist. Whenever trouble flares up anywhere in the world, he's the first correspondent to be parachuted in and all that. Rather him than me, that's all I can say.'

Janna lowered her gaze to her note, but Mrs Parsons' neat handwriting danced madly in front of her eyes.

'Do you remember him, Janna?' Vivien persisted.

'Possibly.' Janna was amazed to hear how calm she sounded. 'But I—I don't remember him being married. How old is the little girl?'

'Seven-ish, I suppose. She'd have to be, for your class. And bright for her age—but then all proud dads think that.'

'I suppose they do,' Janna said automatically, her brain whirling.

'As for him being married,' Vivien's voice lowered confidentially, 'Mrs Parson got the impression that the least said about that the better. I think it was one of these war-time things where no one worried about an actual cere-mony.'

'I see,' Janna said bleakly.

Vivien's eyebrows rose slightly. 'Don't look now, but your disapproval's showing,' she said.

Janna shook her head. 'It isn't entirely that,' she tried to justify herself. 'I was just thinking about Colonel and Mrs Tempest. About how they would have felt—if they'd known.'

Vivien looked at her shrewdly. 'Perhaps they would have reacted more tolerantly than you suppose,' she said. 'Older people are often less extreme in their attitudes than they're given credit for.'

Janna sat down on the edge of the sofa, the unread note still clutched in her hand. 'From what I remember of them, I hardly think so.' She tried to sound casual. 'I think they were both concerned about the apparent decline in moral standards. Neither of them had any sympathy for promi-scuity ...'

'Hold hard!' Vivien sounded a little startled. 'Neither of us knows the true facts. We could be condemning as promiscuous one stable relationship. The fact that there's a child for whom he has assumed the responsibility must surely prove that the affair was deeper than a one-night stand.' She laughed a little uncertainly. 'I don't know why I've been picked for the role of Devil's advocate. I believe in marriage, and I'm sure it's the only successful environment for bringing up children. It's just that I'm surprised to hear someone as young as you sounding so—so ...'

'Intolerant?' Janna supplied rather dryly. 'Well, perhaps I am. I—I just feel so sorry for this little girl, that's all.' She read her note quickly. 'Mrs Parsons thinks she may need extra tuition. She says here there may be a language problem. That Fleur is more fluent in French than in English.' She gave a little groan of dismay. 'That's all I need —a multi-lingual tot!'

Vivien grinned. 'Let her teach the others French,' she

suggested, fastening the belt of her coat. 'No, love, no coffee, thanks. Bill will be sitting at home right now with his tongue hanging out, waiting to be fed. I dare not keep him waiting any longer, or he'll start eating the table mats.'

After Vivien had departed, calling a cheerful goodbye to Mrs Prentiss, Janna walked over to the window and stood staring out into the darkness. It seemed that all her worst forebodings were being realised. Rian had returned, and was back to stay, or so it seemed. Why else would he have sought a place for his child in the local primary school if he did not intend putting down roots of some kind?

Yet what was there for him? she asked herself restlessly. He no longer even had a home here. She shook her head wretchedly, trying to imagine his reaction when he discovered who was planning to live in his former home. There was a terrible irony in the situation. She had caused an irreparable breach between Rian and the only family he had in the world, and by doing so had robbed him of his inheritance. Now she herself was to benefit.

A line from a play—Shakespeare? she wondered tiredly —began to beat in her brain. '*No good can come of this.*'

If Rian had simply contemplated a flying visit back to old haunts, she might have been able to bear it. In many ways, she had been half-expecting it. But the thought of him as a permanent resident in Carrisford, observing her comings and goings, watching her living in his family's house, was not to be borne.

But she would have to bear it unless ... for a brief moment she weighed up the chances of persuading Colin to move elsewhere, then dismissed it as madness. If she even suggested such a thing, he would demand, and be entitled to, a full explanation of her motives, and that she did not feel capable of giving. Besides, she knew he would never agree, no matter how convincing her arguments.

Colin, she thought wryly, knew when he was well off. It was unlikely that he would have got so far so fast with any other firm. She paused abruptly, her hand going to her throat in a little frightened gesture as she realised that this was the first time she had ever admitted this to herself. It was one of the uncomfortable thoughts she had always resolutely pushed away to the back of her mind. Now it had surfaced at last, along with all the others, and could never be relegated again. The diamond on her left hand seemed to glint coldly at her and she shivered. The sensation that all her safe, secure world was falling to pieces around her was stronger than ever. So many things she had never allowed herself to think about, and now they were all jostling for utterance. Her dislike for Colin's father, for instance, with his self-importance and smug satisfaction at his own success, and coupled with this her vague dissatisfaction that Colin had never wanted to cut free and see what he could achieve on his own, without his father's all-pervading influence.

She turned away from the window, crumpling Mrs Parsons' note and sending it spinning on to the fire.

I should never have come back here, she thought despairingly. I'm blaming Colin for what I didn't do myself. I should have struck out on my own. Travelled—I said I always wanted to—taken a job abroad. And unbidden, the traitorous thought came to her mind that she still could.

She groaned aloud. To run away—was that the answer? Once before, she had been a coward, and that was why she was confronted by her present predicament. There was nothing to be gained by running away. She would have to stay and face whatever there was to face. That would be her punishment.

But as she went slowly back upstairs to her room, it chillingly occurred to her that—for Rian—that might not be enough.

It was not a pleasant weekend. On Saturday morning, Janna shopped for her mother, all the time keeping a wary eye open for Rian's car, but she saw no sign of the vehicle or its occupant.

During the afternoon Colin picked her up, and they went

for a drive before returning to his father's house to have dinner. Sir Robert was in one of his most expansive and self-congratulatory moods, and Janna found she was having to work hard to conceal her irritation. He had pulled off some deal concerning shares, and although she did not fully comprehend the ins and outs of the situation, she did gather that this coup had been at the expense of a business rival, and could not join in Colin's obvious enthusiasm for his father's acumen.

When the exquisitely cooked and served meal was over, Sir Robert turned to more personal topics.

'Now that you've found somewhere to live, I suppose you'll be fixing a date?'

'Somewhere to live?' Janna began uncertainly, and Sir Robert, who was lighting a cigar, gave her a sharp look.

'Why, yes. Colin told me he had first refusal on the old Tempest place. A fine house that. Just what you need. And you're to have *carte blanche* in furnishing it. Just choose what you want and send the bills to my secretary. I can't say fairer than that.' He sat back with a pleased air, expelling a cloud of smoke, and waiting to be thanked.

Janna swallowed, avoiding Colin's glance. 'The thing is— I'm not sure ...' she began again.

'Not sure about what?'

Janna was uneasily aware that she had Sir Robert's undivided attention, and that the pleased air had dissipated to some extent. His voice, in fact, held the slight bark which indicated his suspicion that he was about to be told something he did not particularly want to hear. Janna had never personally experienced this before. She had always been treated with a rather fulsome kindness in the past.

Colin came to her rescue as she searched for words.

'Janna isn't totally sold on Carrisbeck House,' he said, sounding deliberately casual.

'And why not, may I ask?' Sir Robert glared at the pair of them, his pleasure in the meal and his cigar destroyed by this strange obduracy. 'It's a fine property, and the fishing rights go with it. What's the matter with it, I'd like to know?'

'Nothing,' Janna answered desperately. She moistened her lips. 'You see, I knew the Tempests, and the thought of living in their old home—and the size of the place—rather overwhelms me, that's all.'

'Oh.' Sir Robert digested this for a moment. 'Well, you're going to be a Travers, my girl, so you'll have to learn not to be overwhelmed.'

'Janna knows that, Dad,' Colin broke in soothingly. 'But I don't want to rush her into anything she's not happy about, so I've given her a few days to come round in her own way.'

'Fair enough, I suppose.' Sir Robert sounded slightly mollified. 'But don't take weeks over it, lass, or some fly character will be in ahead of you.'

For one moment Janna was tempted to ask Sir Robert if he had known Rian, or if he was aware he was back in the locality, but she remained silent. Any such reference on her part could lead to precisely the sort of cross-examination she most wanted to avoid, she thought.

She spent the evening watching television in a desultory manner while Colin allowed his father to beat him at chess.

Later, as Colin drove her home, she sat quietly beside him, hoping against hope that he would not raise the subject of the house again. But she was disappointed. As the car slid to a halt before her gate, Colin said almost too casually, 'I shall have to let Barry know about the Tempest place by Monday, Janna. You'd better let me have your decision one way or another tomorrow.'

'Your father seems to think there's only one decision to be made,' she said, trying to smile.

'Oh, you know Dad.' He was silent for a minute. 'Besides, he has rather a vested interest in the place, I'm afraid.'

'I don't really see why.'

'No.' Colin paused again and then said ruefully, 'I'll have to tell you, darling. He's already had an architect to look

at the place and draw up some plans to convert the old
stables and garage block into a luxury flat for himself. Says
his house is too big now that he's on his own. Wants to be
near us—and his grandchildren.'

Janna's mouth was suddenly dry. 'I see.'

'Do you, darling?' He drew her into his arms and kissed
her, but for the first time in their relationship, she was incapable of more than a token response. 'I was hoping you
would. He's not getting any younger, after all, and he
wouldn't actually be living *with* us. Mrs Masham would
come with him, to cook for him and look after him
generally.'

Janna shook her head. 'I can see he has it all worked out,'
she said more calmly than she felt.

Inwardly, she was seething with anger. This—this was
moral blackmail, she told herself. If she turned Carrisbeck
House down now, it would seem as if she was doing it
because she did not want her future father-in-law living on
the premises. She bit her lip. She had been surprised by the
uncharacteristic generosity of his offer to furnish the house.
Sir Robert had never believed in throwing what he termed
'good brass' about on anything which did not directly concern himself or his own comfort. Now she understood the
motive behind the offer, she would rather live with bare
boards and orange boxes than accept, she thought, her
temper mounting.

'Janna?' Colin's voice was questioning, his mouth persuasive against her ear. 'You wouldn't really mind, would
you, darling? An old man's whim? He may not even go
through with it. And he's very fond of you, you know.'

She gave an edged smile, disengaging herself from his
arms. 'I'll take your word for it,' she answered quietly. 'I
won't pretend that this hasn't been a shock, Colin. I had no
idea your father was thinking along these lines ... However,
you'd better go along with the purchase, as it's what you
both want.'

'But you have to want it too.' He turned her face to his,
his eyes searching hers worriedly.

'I've agreed, haven't I?' she said steadily. 'I won't go back on it.'

'I know you won't.' He took her hand and carried it to his lips. 'That's one of the wonderful things about you, Janna. You're so dependable.'

'Or so predictable?' she questioned dryly. 'I didn't used to be like that Colin. Beware, I might revert to type.'

He laughed, relieved at the apparent lightening of the atmosphere between them. 'I don't think there's much chance of that,' he said carelessly. He kissed her again. 'Goodnight, my love, and dream of me.'

Mrs Prentiss was alone in the sitting room watching a horror film on television as Janna let herself in.

'Hallo, dear, had a nice evening?' she queried automatically as her daughter entered the room, and without a pause, 'I can't understand these people at all, Janna. The villagers have warned them to stay away from the castle, and yet they're all going to spend the night there. It beats me why they're so daft.'

'Why do you watch it then, if that's what you feel?' Janna sat down beside her mother and cast a tolerant eye at the cobwebbed horrors being depicted on the screen.

'I love Christopher Lee,' Mrs Prentiss confessed, reaching for another peppermint cream.

Janna had to smile in spite of herself. She forced herself to sit and watch as the heroine's friend succumbed to the vampire's lure, then, trying to sound casual, she said, 'Mum, when you were engaged, did you have—doubts?'

Mrs Prentiss wrenched her attention away from the bloodstained goings-on in front of her with an obvious effort. 'About your dad?' she exclaimed. 'I don't think so. Why do you ask?'

'No reason,' Janna said uncomfortably. 'I'm just— interested, that's all.'

Her mother surveyed her. 'Are you having second thoughts about marrying Colin?' she demanded. 'Because, if so, you want your head seeing to. The trouble with young people today is that you want everything perfect all the time. You're not prepared to work at a relationship. Have you quarrelled?'

'Oh, no!' Janna was aghast. 'Please, Mum, let's drop the subject.'

'Well, you raised it in the first place,' Mrs Prentiss pointed out reasonably. She leaned forward and switched off the television set. 'Now, let's have this out. Are you having second thoughts about Colin, and if you are, why?'

Janna bit her lip. 'It's nothing as definite as that,' she said miserably. Swiftly she told her mother about Colin's wish to buy Carrisbeck House, and Sir Robert's plan to live in the stable block.

Her mother seemed unimpressed, however. 'It's a modern thing, this wanting to live away from your family,' she remarked. 'When I was a girl, people had their parents to live with them and thought nothing about it. And he won't actually be in the house. I don't see what you're making all the fuss about. Colin is all he's got, after all, and for all his money, he's a lonely man, I daresay.'

'You think I'm being selfish,' Janna said forlornly.

'Not altogether, but I think you're crossing your bridges before you come to them,' Mrs Prentiss said bracingly. 'As Colin said, he may change his mind. And it's a lovely house. There was a time when we couldn't keep you away from there. Not many young people have a chance to start their married life in those circumstances, you know. Look at it from Colin's point of view. And what have you got against the place, anyway?'

It would have been an immense consolation to put her head down on her mother's lap and sob out the whole wretched truth, but Janna could not permit herself that indulgence. Her mother did not deserve to be upset like that after all this time, she thought wearily. The time for confession was long past.

She forced a smile and rose to her feet. 'Nothing, of course. You're right, Mum, I'm sure you are. It's just bridal nerves, I suppose.' She bent and kissed her swiftly.

'Now watch the rest of your film. I'm going to bed before I get nightmares!'

She had not arranged to see Colin on Sunday, and spent a quiet day, lazing round the house, acting her normal self for all she was worth, conscious of the occasional worried glance from her mother. She slept badly that night and rose late on Monday morning, feeling as if she had not rested at all. She was helping her mother strip the beds ready for the weekly wash, when the phone rang.

'Colin?' she said in surprised response to the terse tones at the other end of the line. 'What a strange time to ring. Is anything wrong?'

'Oh, no.' Colin's voice was heavy with sarcasm. 'Everything is for the best in this best of all possible worlds. I just thought you'd like to know that the supreme sacrifice will not be demanded from you after all.'

'What are you talking about?'

'You won't have to live in Carrisbeck House, my sweet. It's been snapped up by someone else while you were dithering about last Friday.' His voice sharpened. 'Hello—Janna—are you still there?'

'Yes, I'm still here,' she managed. 'Colin, I don't know what to say. I'm so sorry. I know how you'd set your heart on it. Do you know—have you any idea who it is?'

'Of course I know.' He gave a short, savage laugh. 'It's in safe hands, darling. Back safely in the bosom of the Tempest family, just as you secretly wished. The Colonel's nephew—Rian or whatever his damned name is—has come back, and he's bought it.'

CHAPTER THREE

JANNA replaced the telephone receiver and stood for a moment, her knuckles pressed childishly against her teeth. She felt totally shaken, not merely by Colin's news, but by the anger and petulance he had displayed in the telling of it.

She had tried to console him, in spite of her own inner turmoil, by telling him that there would be another house for them, but her efforts had been useless. Colin had wanted Carrisbeck House and had been thwarted, and the frustration revealed a totally new side of his character.

She went into the sitting room and sank down on to the sofa, feeling limp. In some ways she could understand his reaction. To many people in Carrisford and the neighbouring villages, Colin and his father were still mere newcomers to be tolerated rather than dales people. Colin, she was sure, had felt that his acquisition of Carrisbeck House would have altered this—that he would in time fill the position in the community that Colonel Tempest once had done. But Janna was not so sure about this. She wondered even if Colin's motives might not have been fully comprehended and resented by the local people. At any rate, such speculation was now a waste of time. Colin would have to find a new way of establishing himself as the new 'squire'.

And if Colin himself was so peevish in his disappointment, she shuddered to think what Sir Robert would say. The only glimmer of brightness in the dark cloud that seemed to be descending on her was that she did not have to face having her future father-in-law living in such close proximity.

Now there was her mother to tell. This was another prospect that Janna did not relish. Mrs Prentiss would undoubtedly want to know why Janna had not informed her that Rian was back and with a small child in tow, who was actually going to be Janna's pupil. Janna sighed. That was how her mother would see it—a piece of interesting and slightly scandalous news to be imparted over the coffee cups. She would certainly not understand why Janna had kept it to herself.

Janna could not fully understand it herself. It would have been so much simpler that way—to mention it casually in passing. 'Oh, by the way, guess who's back?' Now it was too late, and by her silence she had invested Rian's return with an importance that her mother's shrewdness was unlikely to overlook.

But these were minor worries compared with the actuality of Rian's presence as a permanent resident in Carrisford. Of all the places in the world that he had visited, what had drawn him back here to this quiet market town in the shadow of the Pennines? How could he bear to come back to all the memories that Carrisford must evoke, and live in the house from which he had been dismissed in disgrace? When it became generally known that he had been forced to buy his uncle's house and not inherit it as in the normal course of events, she knew that speculation would be rife. And all eyes would be on him anyway because of the child Fleur. He had not always regarded public opinion with such arrogance, she told herself unhappily.

She got up with sudden resolution. No matter what the cost, she would have to see Rian—try and persuade him to change his mind. Could she make him see that no purpose could be served by him living here? If he wanted his revenge on her, then he had already achieved that, by effectively destroying her peace of mind.

She found her suede coat and tugged on matching knee-length boots, then called to her mother that she was going to the library, snatching up a couple of books from the sideboard.

As she walked hurriedly down the long sloping street that led to the market place, she wondered what she would do if Rian was not staying at the White Hart after all, but a swift glance at the hotel car park before she passed under the archway leading to the hotel entrance reassured her. That exotic-looking foreign car he had been driving was there, so he could not be too far away.

The glamorous Barbara Kenton who had once caused her such heart-searchings had vanished from the reception desk long ago and was now reputed to be working as a night-club hostess in Leeds, and the young girl who now filled the job of receptionist looked doubtful when Janna, in a voice she tried hard to make calm, asked for Rian.

No, the girl admitted when pressed, she hadn't *seen* him go out, but breakfast was over a long time ago and he didn't spend much time in the hotel. At last, Janna managed to elicit Rian's room number from her, and said that she would check for herself. She was aware that the girl was watching her with interest as she crossed the small foyer and went up the stairs to the first floor.

At the top, she paused and took a steadying breath, aware that her heart was beating with unusual violence. Her mouth was dry and the palms of her hands felt suddenly clammy. It would not have taken much persuasion for her to have turned and run back the way she had come, but she knew that was impossible. She had to conquer her feelings—see Rian and find out what he intended.

Once before, she thought helplessly. Once before she had climbed a flight of stairs to seek Rian's room—a search that had ended in disaster for them both. It was the memory of that night and its consequences that made her hand shake as she knocked hesitantly on his door.

It opened so swiftly that she was caught completely off guard, her lips parted and her eyes wide and startled. Rian Tempest, tall and lean in faded blue jeans and a dark roll-collared sweater, stood looking down at her. A mirthless smile twisted his mouth, lending no warmth to his dark face or the bleakness of his eyes.

'Come in, Janna.' With an over-elaborate wave of his

hand he invited her to precede him into the room. 'What kept you?'

She hesitated, then walked swiftly past him, her head bent, unnerved by the knowledge that he had been expecting her. Colin had apparently been right with his implication that she was predictable, she thought.

She looked uncertainly round the room, catching her lips in her teeth as she noted the double bed, neatly made under its candlewick coverlet. Was there any significance in this? she wondered. Perhaps Rian being here alone was just a temporary thing. After all, Fleur had a mother, and no one locally knew what her relationship with Rian was at present.

Rian saw where her glance was directed and his smile widened unpleasantly.

'Nervous, Janna?' he inquired. 'You have no need to be, you know. The burned child fears the fire—remember?'

The colour rose in her pale face. 'No,' she began. 'You're mistaken—I don't ...'

'Am I?' His voice was sceptical. 'Perhaps I'd better leave the bedroom door open. Then the chambermaid will hear you—if you feel obliged to scream "Rape!".'

She shuddered convulsively. 'Don't say that word!'

'Why not?' he asked harshly. 'You did—once. Or did you think that might have slipped my memory? I can assure you it hasn't.'

'No, I didn't think that,' she said wearily. 'May—may I sit down?'

'If you want.' He gestured towards two rather uncomfortable-looking easy chairs drawn up on either side of a small electric fire set in the wall. 'May I take your coat?'

She shook her head, giving a slight unconscious shiver. Rian's lips tightened as he regarded her, then he walked past her to the small meter beside the fire and fed a couple of coins into it before switching it on. The bars began to glow almost at once, and he turned back to her.

'Better?' he asked ironically.

'Thank you.' Rather helplessly aware that she no longer

had any excuse to keep it on, Janna unfastened her coat and slipped it from her shoulders before sitting down. She knew that Rian's eyes were going over her, taking in the plain grey flannel skirt, and the simple round-necked pale pink sweater she wore with it.

'My God,' he observed after a moment. 'The transformation into the country schoolma'am is almost complete. Who would have thought it?'

She flushed again, pushing back some strands of dark hair which had fallen forward on to her cheek.

'Yes,' he went on, 'the change is quite remarkable. Forgive me if I dwell upon it, but I'm trying to reconcile your present image with the one you presented at our last eventful meeting. It's—not easy.'

He walked over to the table beside the bed and extracted a cigar from a silver case. He lit the cigar before returning to the fire, and flinging himself into the chair opposite her. He blew out a cloud of smoke and studied her through it with half-closed eyes.

'Whatever happened to her, I wonder—that girl in the white lace trouser suit and damned little else who danced like an amalgam of Salome and Cleopatra? Has your estimable fiancé ever been permitted to catch a glimpse of her, or have you buried her for ever under an avalanche of cashmere and tweed and sensible shoes?'

'Oh, please.' Janna pressed her fingers against her hot cheeks. 'Can we leave Colin out of this discussion?'

His brows rose. 'Is that possible? I wouldn't have thought so—under the circumstances. But perhaps I've misunderstood the motivation for this visit.'

Their eyes met and Janna's glance was the first to fall away.

'I don't think so,' she said lamely. 'You—you must be able to guess why I'm here.'

His eyes narrowed. 'I'm not in the mood for guessing games, Janna,' he said succinctly. 'And you weren't always so reticent about your feelings. Suppose you tell me just what's going on in that devious little mind of yours.'

Desperately she moistened her lips. 'Rian, why have you come back?' The words came out in a frightened little rush. 'Is it—does it have anything to do with me?'

There was a brief pause, then he laughed, a soft, jeering sound which nevertheless held a note of menace that chilled her.

'Why, yes, sweet witch.' The words were light, but not so the tone they were uttered in. 'But then you never really doubted that for a moment, did you?'

She shrank back into her chair, gripping the wooden arms so hard that her knuckles turned white.

Her voice shaking, she said, 'What are you going to do?'

Reflectively, he studied the glowing tip of his cigar.

'Now that I haven't decided yet. When I do come to a decision, you will be the first to know, I promise you, Janna. In the meantime, it won't do you any harm to be on tenter-hooks for a little while.'

She leaned forward, her eyes pleading with him. 'Do you suppose I haven't been—for the past seven years?'

'Poor Janna.' He gave a careless shrug. 'But if you knew that I'd come looking for you eventually, then why are you still here?'

'Because I couldn't think of anywhere else to go,' she said unevenly. 'I couldn't think of anywhere I would be safe.'

'Your instinct was right, of course.' He drew deeply once more on the cigar before crushing it out in the ashtray be-side his chair. 'Wherever you had run to, I would have found you in the end.'

'I didn't mean simply safe from you,' she said wearily. 'I—I had to be safe from myself as well.'

He laughed sardonically. 'So you decided the only safety was in staying and facing the music, whenever it came. I congratulate you, Janna. The little girl grew up at last and found her courage. Hang on to that courage, sweet witch. You're going to need every last ounce of it by the time I've done with you.'

She bowed her head defeatedly. 'Oh, Rian, have mercy on me,' she whispered wretchedly.

'Following your own example, no doubt.' His voice lashed at her. 'No, Janna. I've entertained a number of feelings towards you over the years, but I can't say that mercy has ever been among them. You'll take my medicine, darling, in whatever dosage I dictate to you.'

She got up, stumbling a little in her haste, feeling the tears pricking the back of her eyelids and wanting to escape from that suddenly stifling room before they overwhelmed her. She reached for her coat, but Rian was there before her, plucking it from the back of the chair and holding it for her to put on with a smile that told her he understood quite well this sudden urge of hers to be gone.

Biting her lip, she thrust her arms into the sleeves, and felt him slide the garment on to her shoulders. She wanted with every breath in her body to walk away from him to the door, but his hands remained on her shoulders, compelling her to be still. Then, as she stiffened in sudden outrage, he let his hands slide forwards down her body, lingering over the soft roundness of her breasts.

'Your clothes may have changed, Janna, but your body hasn't.' His voice was wicked against her ear. 'Not all my memories of you are unhappy ones, you see.'

She wrenched herself free with an incoherent cry and swung round on him, her hand flying up instinctively to strike at his face. But he parried the intended blow with consummate ease, catching her wrist in a grip which caused her to cry out in pain.

'I don't advise it,' he said coolly. 'I doubt if you're pre-pared for the sort of retribution I should exact.'

He released her hand almost contemptuously and she stood, staring up at him and rubbing her numbed wrist where the marks of his fingers showed plainly. He was looking at her hand.

'That's a beautiful ring you're wearing, Janna. A man would have to think a great deal of a woman to invest in that sort of ice. I would give it back to him, sweet witch. Far more dignified than making him have to ask you for it.'

'You swine!' she said between her teeth, and he laughed for the first time with a note of genuine amusement.

'That's more like the Janna I used to know. I thought she was dead when you came here asking for mercy instead of spitting in my eye as you would have done once, and daring me to do my worst.' She turned angrily to the door, but he detained her. 'You've surprised me today, Janna. When you arrived, I thought you'd come on behalf of your fiancé, to add your weight to his plea to me to give up Carrisbeck House in his favour.'

'Colin did that?' Janna gasped. 'I don't believe you.'

He shrugged. 'Ask him,' he advised. 'He won't have forgotten the conversation. I doubt whether he's ever offered anyone so much money in his life before and been refused.' He lifted a sardonic brow at her. 'When you showed up, I thought for one optimistic minute that he might be sending in the big guns. Getting you with your womanly wiles'— he let his glance drift significantly towards the big bed— 'to achieve what he with his money could not. Life is full of these little disappointments.'

'You're vile. Colin wouldn't do such a thing.'

'No? I wouldn't count on it. From my brief dealings with him, I get the strongest impression that he'd be willing to sell his own grandmother to get what he wanted. I don't think even you would be wise to try his chivalry too far.'

'You know nothing about Colin,' she said, her voice shaking.

He laughed. 'And does he know anything about you? I doubt it. In fact, I'm counting on it.'

Before she could guess what he was going to do, he had reached out for her with long arms, pulling her against him so that their bodies were locked together. For a moment she knew panic, then his mouth came down on hers, hard and demanding, and the world whirled into a chaos where his kiss was the only reality.

It was as if the wellsprings of her emotions, dammed up for seven years, had been suddenly released. Her mouth parted helplessly under the pressure of his, and her hands crept up involuntarily to lock themselves behind his dark head as his lips explored hers with an arrogant intimacy that promised nothing short of total possession.

And then, as suddenly and shockingly as it had begun, it was over. Her hands were wrenched free and he was thrusting her away from him with a force that nearly made her overbalance.

His hair was dishevelled, and he raked his fingers carelessly through it, as he stood watching her with a cynical assessment that acted like a deluge of cold water on her awakened senses. He seemed totally unmoved by what had just passed between them, she thought dazedly, as if his sole concern had simply been to arouse her desires without becoming in the least involved himself. But even as she rejected the idea violently, his own words confirmed it.

'I was right, you see, Janna.' His voice was cool, his face expressionless. 'You really haven't changed at all.'

She gave a little choking cry of protest, then turned and fled out of the room.

Just along the corridor before she reached the stairs she glimpsed the white porcelain gleam of a bathroom through a half-open door, and dived into it, slamming the door behind her and sliding the bolt across. But there were no sounds of pursuit from the corridor. He had let her go—for now at least.

It was only a small room, containing a huge old-fashioned bath with gleaming brass taps, and a wash-basin. A high-backed chair with a wooden seat had been placed under the frosted glass window, and Janna made her way to it unsteadily and sat down. She had caught a glimpse of herself in the mirror above the basin as she passed, and had winced as she had done so. What had happened to the cool, self-contained creature she had built up so successfully over the years? She bore no relation to the girl she had seen in the mirror, with her wild, enormous eyes, and mouth blurred and swollen with passion.

She folded her arms tightly across her breasts, fighting back the little moan that threatened to rise to her lips. Oh God, what had she done? Why hadn't she been able to foresee the inherent dangers in going to appeal to Rian? All she had achieved was to reveal to him the full extent of her vulnerability—something she had not even been aware of herself until then, and the awareness had shaken her to the core of her being.

One of her consolations over the past seven years had lain in telling herself that she could not be blamed for the errors of adolescence and that her all-devouring passion for Rian and its disastrous aftermath could only be included in this category. But now she had no such excuse to explain how one calculated insult of a kiss could set her body alight. She wasn't a child any longer, playing with fire. She was a woman and in imminent danger of being consumed by the blaze she herself had re-kindled.

She gripped her hands together tightly, feeling the hardness of Colin's ring biting into her flesh. How could she have let herself behave like that when she was engaged— promised body and soul to another man? she asked herself despairingly. She had betrayed Colin as surely as if she had allowed Rian to lift her on to his bed and take possession of her body.

She shivered. Her weakness, her lack of self-control— of decency even, she lashed herself—had simply given Rian another weapon to use against her when it pleased him to do so.

Hadn't he given her full warning that he intended to destroy her relationship with Colin in one way or another? Her only refuge seemed to lie in confessing frankly to Colin what had happened, not simply today, but seven years ago before Rian could tell him first.

She stared dully at the brightly patterned vinyl floor-covering at her feet. She had to face the fact that Rian's warning might not be so far from the truth. She simply did not know how Colin would react. She had never had to test the strength of his feeling for her, or his forgiveness, and disturbingly she was aware that the realisation gave her no feeling of confidence.

She had known almost from the start that Colin, although attracted by her, would not have started wooing her if she had not been what his father would term 'suitable'. In the world they moved in, such things mattered, and she was sure that Sir Robert had forgiven the fact that she did not come from a wealthy family solely on the grounds of her utter respectability. Her father was the Chief Planning Officer with the district council, and her mother was a leading light in the Women's Institute, and the local charity organisations. There had never been a breath of scandal associated with any of their names. Until now.

She leaned back against the unyielding support of the chair and closed her eyes, letting her mind drift back again to that distant summer, almost welcoming the pain that memory brought in its wake.

It was all there—newly alive, newly awakened by those brief moments in Rian's arms. Moments she had desperately spent a whole portion of her life reassuring herself would never be repeated.

It was gratitude that had caused Mrs Tempest to invite Janna to the party at Carrisbeck House. She knew that. It had all been part of a carefully worked out campaign. If Rian was avoiding her then she would get to him somehow through his aunt. That was why she had spent one long and incredibly boring afternoon manning the White Elephant stall for which Mrs Tempest was responsible at the annual summer fête. All her friends who were helping had volunteered to sell cakes or home-made produce—things that were quickly sold out, releasing them to enjoy themselves for the rest of the afternoon. There was never any chance of that with White Elephants. There was always a fair proportion of these left at the end of the afternoon, to be taken away and stored in someone's attic until the next time.

Mrs Tempest was quite aware of this, and she realised it was a sacrifice for Janna on this hot and perspiring afternoon. Thus, she was grateful. And thus, the invitation to the party the following week.

Janna was not in the least perturbed to realise that she would undoubtedly be the youngest person at the party, and her confidence hoped to overcome any lingering scruples her parents might have had. She was also buoyed up by the certain knowledge that Barbara Kenton had not been invited. Rian might find her an amusing way of passing his leisure time, but he would not inflict her on his uncle and aunt.

And then there was the trouser suit. The moment she had seen it in the boutique she had known she must have it, and she had secretly drawn money out of her savings account to pay for it. It was at the back of her wardrobe now, and the only problem was how she was going to get out of the house in it without being sent back upstairs by her mother to change into something more suitable.

Mrs Prentiss might be easy-going in some ways, but Janna knew what her reaction would be to clinging hipster pants in white crochet lace, and a long-sleeved jacket top which left the midriff bare and hardly covered the wearer's breasts. She had experimented with different ways of doing her hair, and had decided to sweep it all into a loose knot on top of her head, and secure it with a white artificial rose. She had bought new make-up too—silver eyeshadow and a pale lipstick which made her mouth shimmer like pearl.

When she was dressed on the night of the party, she caught her breath as she studied herself in the long mirror on the back of her wardrobe door. It was no child that looked back at her, but a young woman, provocative and sensuous, knowing what she wanted and how to go about getting it.

She got out of the house and into the waiting taxi without difficulty. Her mother was in the kitchen preparing refreshments for a committee meeting later that evening, and her father was at the rear of the house, spraying his roses.

She was numb with tension all the way to the house. He had been in London the previous week. What if he had decided to return there, and skip the party altogether? Or even worse, what if he had invited one of his sophisticated London girl-friends to be there with him? Janna squared her shoulders under the flimsy lace covering, and lifted her chin defiantly. Her mirror had told her that she didn't have to be afraid of competition from anyone that night.

Sweet witch, he had called her mockingly. Well, tonight she would make it true. She would bewitch Rian so that he would never mock her again. He had admitted he was attracted to her. Tonight, he would find her irresistible.

She found, when she entered the drawing room, that she knew most of the people there, and that the trouser suit which had seemed the ultimate in daring at home was not nearly so extreme compared with the models being worn by some of the girls. She was glad not to be too conspicuous. She did not want any tales to be carried back to her mother.

She looked round, trying to be casual, searching for Rian among the laughing, chattering groups of people, but she could not see him, and for a moment she was bleakly afraid that all her worst forebodings had been realised. Then she heard someone call to him, and realised with a rush of relief that he was merely out on the terrace.

She stepped out through the french doors, smiling shyly in reply to the people who greeted her. Rian was in the centre of a boisterous group. As Janna hesitated, he turned away laughing to put his empty glass on the terrace parapet beside him, and saw her. For a moment his eyes narrowed almost disbelievingly. The palms of her hands were clammy with sweat. If he laughed at her now, she thought hysterically, if he made even one joke, then she would kill herself.

But there was not the faintest amusement in his dark face as he came swiftly to her side. His hand seemed to burn her flesh as he took her arm, drawing her aside, away from the other people to where a climbing rose spilled its perfume on to the grey flags.

'Janna?' His voice held a question, a faint bewilderment, and she knew a feeling of triumph.

'Rian.' She smiled up into his eyes, holding them with her own, and heard him draw a sharp breath. Then he smiled too, but without mockery.

'I don't know what you've done to yourself,' he said quietly, 'but I want you to know you're very lovely. Like a bud that has suddenly come to bloom.'

She felt the colour steal up under her skin, and hated herself for her lack of poise.

Rian put up his hand and brushed her warm cheek gently with his fingers.

'And the blush makes it perfection,' he said. She thought for one heart-stopping minute that he was going to say something else, and then someone from the group he had left shouted to him, and he half-turned.

'I must go,' he said abruptly. 'But I'll claim a dance with you later, if I may.'

She held her delight severely in check, murmuring that she would look forward to it.

From that moment on, she was never alone for a minute. The dancing began in the big hall soon after that, and she was never without a partner. At any other time she would have relished her triumph, knowing full well that other girls, older than herself and more expensively dressed, were watching from the sidelines, yet her success all seemed meaningless, because Rian was not among the endless succession of young men vying to dance with her.

She began to feel desperate again. The evening was half over and Rian had not come near her since that first moment. Where was he, and why hadn't he kept his promise to dance with her? No one else mattered. She'd had countless offers to take her home, to take her out to dinner, to take her driving, and she had kept them all laughingly at arms' length, because she was waiting for Rian.

Supper was served around ten o'clock, but Janna could hardly eat a thing. At any other time the chilled asparagus rolls, the *vol au vents*, the exquisitely garnished platters of meat would have enchanted her. She ate dutifully, and laughed and talked, but all the time her eyes were darting searching glances to every corner of the big dining room. Oh, where was he? Why didn't he come?

At last she could stand it no longer, and with a murmured excuse she left her group and went back into the hall. A few couples were sitting on the stairs, chatting quietly, but Rian was not among them. He was not in the drawing room either, and quietly she went across to the french doors and on to the terrace. For a moment she thought it was deserted, and then in the far corner she saw a tall, familiar figure silhouetted against the last remnants of daylight.

She went up to him and touched his arm. He turned sharply to face her, and she saw with a twinge of alarm that he was frowning heavily. When he saw who it was, his brow cleared slightly and he made an obvious effort to be welcoming.

'Why aren't you eating with the rest of them?' he asked. 'Don't tell me you're watching your figure already?'

'Do I need to?' Mischievously, she twirled round for his benefit. But he did not answer her smile. The brooding look had returned to his dark face.

'No,' he said briefly, 'you don't need to. Go back indoors, Janna. It's getting chilly out here, and they're starting the dancing again.'

'That's precisely why I'm here,' she said, trying to recapture the lighthearted mood of earlier in the evening. 'You said you'd dance with me, and you've been nowhere near me.'

'I didn't think my absence would be noticed when you

had so many round you,' he said dryly, and her heart leaped, as she thought, 'Perhaps he's jealous.'

'Of course I noticed,' she said gaily. 'A promise is a promise, after all.'

He hesitated. 'I'm not in a dancing mood, Janna. You'll have to forgive me for tonight.'

She could have wept with disappointment and frustration. All evening she had been waiting for this. It had been the culmination of all her planning, all her hopes, and now it was to be denied her. Or was it? Not if she knew it.

She lifted her chin. 'Very well, my lord. Then your handmaiden will dance for you.'

The music from the hall drifted through, the beat slow, heavy and rhythmical.

At first she had intended it as a joke, an attempt to jolt him out of this strange introspective mood. She'd expected him to laugh and capitulate and take her into the hall and dance with her. But he did not. He stood and watched her as she circled and swayed in front of him, and gradually she became aware of a growing intentness in his gaze—a new and disturbing tension that had entered the atmosphere between them. She began to follow the beat of the music more closely, moved her feet less and her hips more, acting on pure instinct. Her lips felt dry and she moistened them with the tip of her tongue and saw her action was not lost on him. As the music rose to its climax, she placed her hands behind her head, arching her body towards him with deliberate provocation.

'God in heaven,' he said unsteadily. 'Janna—you ...'

There were no more words. He pulled her towards him, crushing the softness of her breasts against his hard body, kissing her passionately and demandingly without regard for her total inexperience of such an embrace. For a moment she was shocked. Her innocence had not prepared her for this, then suddenly, instinctively, the woman in her took over, and she was responding at first shyly and then with

a warmth and ardour she had not dreamed she was capable
of.

As she had danced, she had let her hands slide down her
body. Now his hands followed the same path, and everywhere he touched, her nerve-endings awoke to a quivering
vibrancy. Unashamedly she pressed herself against him,
recognising his arousal and glorying in it.

This was the only witchcraft between a man and a
woman, she thought, her head reeling. This demand, this
longing to touch and be touched, to kiss and be kissed, to
know and be known.

At last he raised his head, and his arms fell away from
her. She swayed towards him.

'Rian,' she murmured, the ache of wanting unmistakable
in her voice.

'Janna!' His hands descended sharply on her shoulders,
deliberately holding her away from him. His face was white
under his tan, and his dark eyes seemed to burn as he
looked down at her. 'This is madness and we both know it.
You're a child, and you don't know what you're doing.'

'Then teach me.' Her voice shook.

'No!' he said with sudden violence. 'You don't know what
you're asking. You're a virgin, Janna, totally innocent, so
don't try and pretend otherwise. And don't ask me to
destroy that innocence. Keep it as a precious gift for the
man you'll marry one day.'

He let her go abruptly and turned and walked away from
her into the lamp-lit brilliance of the drawing room. Janna
stood alone in the darkness, totally bereft, a taste of blood
in her mouth. But as coherent thought began to return, one
thing dominated. Rian wanted her, as completely as a man
could want a woman, and it was only some quixotic notion
of chivalry which had stopped him from taking her. He'd
thought her simply carried away by her feelings, overwhelmed by her first experience of adult lovemaking. She
would prove to him that she was in deadly earnest, and
that her desires matched his.

She went through the darkened hall, where a few couples swayed in each other's arms oblivious to everything else, and up the stairs. No one noticed her, or if they did, they drew the obvious conclusion that she was looking for the bathroom.

On the landing, she paused, nerving herself. She had no idea which was Rian's room, but she had no doubt that her instinct would take her to it, or that she would find him there. Cool reason suggested he had gone to seek privacy in which to regain his self-control.

The enigmatically closed doors gave her no clue whatsoever, but she knew just the same. The carved knob twisted easily under her fingers, and she walked into the room.

Rian was standing at the window, smoking a cigarette. He had discarded his jacket and loosened his tie. He swung round at the sign of the opening door, and she saw that he was frowning.

'Janna,' he said, and his voice was grim. 'I'm warning you, go away from me now. Go back downstairs before something happens that we'll both regret.'

'I shan't regret anything,' she said steadily. 'Rian, I—I've brought you a gift. Don't you want it?'

Her fingers shook slightly as she unfastened the flimsy crochet top, and let it fall to the floor.

He took one deep, unsteady breath and then his cigarette went flying out through the open window, and he came to her.

She clung to him without reserve as he lifted her on to his bed.

'I've been wondering all night what you could possibly wear under that fragment.' A laugh tore at his voice. 'Now I know.'

He bent and kissed her breasts, his mouth warm and urgent on her body, and yet at the same time she knew that he was deliberately restraining himself, devoting himself to her pleasure, her arousal, so that when the time came she would have no fear of him.

'God, I've wanted you,' he whispered. He took the pins out of her hair, letting it tumble on to her shoulders. He lifted a handful of dark strands and held them against his face.

She drew his head down to her, offering him her lips, and he took them fiercely.

At last he muttered raggedly against her mouth, 'Janna, my love, my sweet witch, you're wearing too many clothes, do you know that?'

She knew that even then he was giving her the chance, if she wished, to change her mind. But she did not wish.

'So are you,' she whispered in return. She slid her hands under his unfastened shirt, enjoying the unfamiliar warmth of his bare skin.

The sudden blaze of light in the room was intrusion enough. Mrs Tempest's voice, unnaturally high-pitched and agitated, crying out, 'Rian—good God!' was a sickening, mind-numbing shock.

Janna felt Rian roll away from her on to his back, his hand shielding his eyes from the sudden dazzle of the lights. His aunt was standing near the door, her hand still on the light-switch. The Colonel stood behind her.

For a second, Janna was too terrified to move, then she snatched at the coverlet, pulling it across her body.

'What the devil is the meaning of this?' The Colonel's voice was thunderous with anger. 'How dare you, sir! How dare you turn your aunt's home into a brothel!. Have you no sense of decency?'

There was a long pause, then Rian said very levelly, 'In future, I'll remember to lock my door.'

'Is that the only answer you can give?' the Colonel roared. 'You disgust me, sir. Do you think I'm blind? I've always known you had the morals of an alley-cat, but I've said nothing, as long as you didn't parade your trollops in front of my wife.'

Janna, half paralysed with shock, realised numbly that he was talking about her ... She saw Mrs Tempest looking at her, and read shock and condemnation in her eyes.

'Janna!' Mrs Tempest shook her head helplessly. 'How could you abuse our hospitality in this way?'

Janna gasped. This was a nightmare. It couldn't be happening. Not to her. Not to Janna Prentiss. Her parents' faces swam across her dazed vision. Her parents who loved her and were proud of her. What would they say, she thought wildly, when she was brought home in such utter disgrace? All their faith in her, their trust would be destroyed. From the moment Rian's arms had closed around her she had not given them a single thought. Now the thought of her mother's face, grieved and outraged, seemed to fill her mind to the exclusion of everything else. It couldn't happen. She wouldn't let it happen.

'No!' she cried hysterically as Mrs Tempest turned to leave the room. 'No—you don't understand. He—Rian brought me here ... I didn't want to—but he made me.' She pointed at the scrap of white crochet lying in the middle of the bedroom carpet. 'He—he tore my top off. I thought he'd gone mad. I—I was frightened. I begged him to stop—but he wouldn't.'

The silence in the room seemed endless. No one seemed to be breathing at all. She couldn't look at Rian—couldn't meet his eyes.

The Colonel found his voice first. 'Are you saying,' he said hoarsely, 'that you were unwilling? That my nephew actually tried to—rape you?'

It was too late now to hedge, or even retract what she had said. She had sown the seeds of the storm and now the whirlwind would follow.

'Yes,' she whispered, and burst into tears, long strangled sobs that tore at her throat. It was the final touch of conviction her story needed. Her youth and her fright would do the rest.

The Colonel was speaking very quietly. 'You'll leave my house in the morning, Rian, and I never want to see your face again. You have disgraced your family and your name,

as well as insulting and terrifying this young girl. I would
send you packing now if the house were not full of our
guests. I have no wish to cause your aunt any further dis-
tress.' He paused. 'Have you nothing to say?'

It was as close, Janna realised afterwards, as the older
man would ever come to asking Rian to deny the whole
thing.

As if in a dream, she heard Rian reply levelly, 'Nothing
at all, sir. It all seems to have been said already—most
comprehensively.'

The Colonel was addressing her now. 'My wife will—
er—assist you, young lady, and see that you get home. We
shall of course say nothing of this to anyone. I realise it is
asking a great deal of your generosity to request that you do
the same. Nevertheless, I am asking it.'

He waited, and accepted her brief, convulsive nod with
a little sigh.

'Tidy yourself, Rian, and come downstairs. We still have
guests. Nothing has happened here, do you understand?
Nothing.'

'Nothing,' Rian repeated. His tone was quiet, almost re-
flective, but the memory of it still had the power to chill
Janna, even seven years later.

She came back to the present with a start as someone
rattled impatiently at the bathroom door. She got up slowly
from the hard chair and walked to the basin, putting in the
plug and running in the cold water.

She glanced at herself in the mirror, noticing almost dis-
passionately her white face and tearstained cheeks. Hardly
any different, she thought, from the girl who had huddled
into her clothes under the cold inimical gaze of Mrs
Tempest. That girl had cried too, partly in relief because
she was safe from her parents' anger, partly in fear, but
most of all in an agony of shame and regret at her own
cowardice.

That girl had had good reason to cry.

'But I have no reason—no reason at all,' she told herself, beginning to splash cold water on to her face. When she had finished, her face was calm again, and the tearstains had disappeared. Only the guilt remained, and the dread, and those she could conceal under her usual composed exterior—at least for the time being, she thought with a wry twist of her mouth.

The question was—just how much longer did she have?

CHAPTER FOUR

IT was raining when she got outside, great leaden drops from an impenetrably grey sky. She stood hesitating under the shelter of the hotel arch, trying to make up her mind to make a dash for it. She had neither headscarf nor umbrella with her, so she had resigned herself to a drenching.

As she stepped forward reluctantly, a large car purred through the puddles already beginning to collect between the cobbles of the market square and drew up beside the kerb in front of her.

The rear door swung open.

'Janna.' Sir Robert's slightly peevish tone came to her ears. 'Don't stand there getting soaked, lass. Get in.'

She had no choice but to comply, although a confrontation with Colin's father was the last thing in the world she would have chosen at that particular moment. Mustering a smile and a brief word of thanks, she climbed in beside him, and sank back into the affluent aroma of leather and good cigars.

He gave the chauffeur his orders, then turned to look at he:

'Well, this is a fine how-d'ye-do, I must say. I warned you what would come of your shilly-shallying, my girl.'

'You've heard, then,' she prevaricated.

'Well, of course I've heard,' he riposted tetchily. 'Who would Colin tell first, if not me, I'd like to know? After all, I did have a personal concern in the matter.'

'So did I,' Janna told him drily, and he sent her an irritated look.

'Now don't start going all feminine on me, Janna—I had enough of that to put up with from Colin's mother, God rest her soul,' he added perfunctorily. 'I never could make

68

her see that in matters of business, she sometimes had to take a back seat. I thought you would have more sense.'

'I'm sorry.' Janna's own irritation was aroused. 'I didn't realise Carrisbeck House was a business proposition. I'd got the impression it was going to be my home.'

'Of course it was going to be your damned home, but you don't imagine I was going to spend that kind of brass, just to put a roof over your head, do you? Colin needs a place like that to entertain our clients. I thought he'd explained all that to you.'

'Yes, he explained,' she acknowledged wearily. 'This conversation seems a little pointless under the circumstances, don't you think?'

'I don't intend to let the matter rest—not by a long chalk.' Sir Robert's usually pugnacious expression took on a look of new determination. 'Everyone has their price. I don't suppose this Tempest chap is any different.'

Janna hesitated. 'I don't think he's interested in money.'

'Then he's a fool.' Sir Robert sent her a narrow look. 'And how is it you're so knowledgeable on the subject?'

There was no point in trying to dodge the issue. Sir Robert had seen her emerging from the White Hart, and was just as capable as the next man, if not more so, of putting two and two together.

'Because I've just been to see him, and he told me Colin had made him an offer—asked him to change his mind. He said he had refused.'

'So you went to see what you could do.' Sir Robert's tone was unexpectedly congratulatory. 'Well, Janna, you've surprised me, lass, I must say. I never thought you had that sort of initiative in you, and I think the more of you for it. Knew him before, did you?' His voice might be casual, but the glance he shot her was anything but.

Janna strove for a light touch. 'Oh, Rian Tempest was one of our childhood gods locally.' She gave a brittle laugh. 'I was just one of a string of tiresome kids trailing round after him. He—he hardly remembered me.'

Another deception, she thought tiredly, for which she would ultimately have to pay. What was the price, she wondered, for buying time?

'And what sort of reaction did you get? Did he strike you that he might become amenable, if the circumstances were right?'

Janna hesitated, but honesty won. 'No, he didn't,' she said at last. 'I got the impression that he wanted the house and means to hang on to it.'

'Damnation,' Sir Robert muttered. 'It's beyond me. If he wanted the house that badly, and his uncle knew it, why the hell didn't the old man leave it to him in his will? It's the obvious course. There's something fishy going on there, Janna, you mark my words, and I mean to get to the bottom of it.'

'Oh no!' The appalled words had escaped before Janna could prevent them. Aware of Sir Robert's eyes, surprised and suddenly suspicious, she sought hurriedly to cover herself. 'I—I'm sure you're wrong. Rian—Rian was doing a very difficult and dangerous job. The Colonel may have felt he might not survive to receive his inheritance. And he was always—independent.'

'Hm.' Sir Robert was clearly not impressed by the lameness of her arguments. He sat in silence for a few moments, staring into space, rousing himself as the car drew up outside Janna's gate. 'Well, here you are, lass, and I've saved you a wetting. Don't bother your head any more about the house. I'll take it from here. I'm not a man who's easily worsted. You'll grant me that, I think.'

Janna woodenly agreed. She had other less charitable ways of expressing it, and she knew a shiver of fear as she watched the car draw away. She felt trapped, caught between Rian's vengeance and Sir Robert's ruthlessness.

And as she walked up the path towards the house, she remembered with a sinking heart that she had left the library books she had taken as an alibi in Rian's hotel room. He had not only won the first round hands down, but she had presented him with a weapon to use against her in the second.

The next few days passed uneventfully, and Janna forced herself to put her personal problems to the back of her mind, and prepare some work for next term. She retrieved the script of her Nativity play from the suitcase on top of the wardrobe, updating it and making a few cuts at the same time. She would have to discuss the choice of carols to go with it with Beth who taught music throughout the school, she thought. Mrs Parsons always preferred them to include at least one modern carol which the children had to learn along with the traditional favourites.

She had already decided to give the children a project in which they found out as much as they could about Christmas in other lands, and she spent some time collecting material for this, and making the big loose-leaf books in which the children would write and draw their findings.

She saw Colin, of course. He took her out for a drink one evening, and another night they went out to dinner at a fifteenth-century inn in a neighbouring village, but it was useless to pretend that everything was just the same between them. For one thing, he never mentioned the house, and when she once tentatively raised the subject, told her dismissively that he did not wish to discuss it any further. Janna was distressed by this. She had no means of knowing whether Sir Robert had told him of her abortive visit to Rian, and what construction had been placed on this. In addition, it made her uneasy to feel that their relationship for the first time contained a no-go area. What would happen once they were married if Colin refused to discuss with her the points on which they were at variance? Would it mean a lifetime of uncomfortable silences? she thought, stealing a glance at his unyielding profile as they drove home one night. She had always described Colin's chin to herself as 'firm'. Now she was beginning ruefully to wonder if 'stubborn' might not be a better description. She had always consoled herself in the past with the thought that Colin must be more like his mother than his father, but now she was no longer so sure. It was as if this business over the house had thrown a whole new and disturbing light over their relationship, and if Colin would not talk to her about it, how could it be resolved?

At her most pessimistic, she told herself that it did not matter anyhow. That whatever she did would be doomed to failure because of Rian, who had the power to destroy their relationship anyway.

That night when Colin took her in his arms, she clung to him, trying to reassure herself.

'Colin, you do still love me?' She could hardly recognise herself in the halting words.

He looked at her, plain astonished. 'Janna.' He bent and kissed her. His mouth was warm and pleasurable, and she returned his kiss with unwonted ardour. For one crazy moment, she found herself hoping that her passion might set light to his own, and that he would lose all control of himself and make love to her. If once she belonged to him completely, a voice argued within her, then she was certain he would never leave her, no matter what might happen. She was sure of him then. Besides, there might be a child to bind them even more closely.

And there was more. Colin's lips, Colin's body might block out all those other memories which had returned to torment her. She was ashamed of the wanton way her senses had yielded to Rian. She tried to convince herself that these adolescent fevers were behind her now, but he had shown her in a few brief moments just how vulnerable she was.

But it was Colin she wanted, she thought wildly. She needed to know that she could respond to him in the same way. That he could set her passion blazing, and provide its ultimate fulfilment.

For one reeling minute, before sanity returned, she could have cried with disappointment as Colin's mouth left hers, and he set her gently but firmly away from him.

'Has that convinced you?' he asked tenderly, and with a hint of indulgence in his voice.

She swallowed. If she obeyed her instinct and said 'no' what would he do? Would he understand? It frightened her to think she could not be sure, and yet she was committed to him.

He touched the curve of her throat caressingly with his forefinger. 'Silly girl! I've chosen you, you know that, and very soon you're going to be my wife.'

'Not that soon.' She spoke constrainedly, conscious of the forbidden topic of the house creating new tension. Before they could be married they had to find somewhere to live —somewhere else to live.

'Sooner than you think.' He pulled her close to him again, resting his lips on her hair. 'I'm sorry I've been a bit of a swine lately, darling. I think it's partly this waiting that's getting me down. Engagements are hell—everyone says so, and I'd really thought that we could set the date at last. It was a hell of a disappointment to—lose out like that. Do you understand?'

'Yes.' Relief flooded through her. How could she have doubted him? she thought, afire with happiness. She put up her hand and stroked his cheek. Her voice was warm and soft as she said, 'But we don't have to wait, Colin. If we love each other, that's all that matters.' She twisted in his arms slightly and looked up at him, trying to ascertain the expression on his face in the dimness of the car. 'Darling, you know what I'm trying to say.'

'Oh, Janna,' he said on a long sigh, and she realised with a pang of dismay that there was no passion in his voice, no jubilance. 'You can't really mean it. At least, I hope you don't. All my life, I've had this ideal. My wife, my bride coming to me down the aisle in white—not because it's the fashionable thing to do, but because white is the—virginal colour. It means so much to me, Janna, knowing that when we're together on our wedding night, it will be for the first time, and that no other man will have touched you as I will. That's why although the waiting is hard, it isn't unbearable, because I know that will be my reward eventually.' He kissed her hair softly. 'Don't tempt me, darling. Don't ask me to do anything that might spoil this dream.'

She sat suddenly rigid in his arms, conscious of feeling humiliated. She had offered herself to Colin, and he had refused.

When she spoke, her voice trembled. 'And you, Colin? When we're together on this ideal—wedding night you have planned—will it be the first time for you as well? Or don't your principles demand male virginity as well?'

He lifted his head sharply and looked down at her. She could sense his displeasure even before he spoke.

'I thought you would also understand, Janna—that you would be mature enough to know that—a certain amount of experience is—necessary for a man.'

'But not for a woman.' Anger allied to the fading humiliation took her out of his arms, and as far away from him as she could get in the car. 'Hurrah for the double standard!'

'Don't be ridiculous,' he said flatly. 'You know as well as I do that there's always far more involved for a woman than there is for a man . . .' He paused as if embarrassed. 'A man can have any number of casual affairs without them meaning very much at all. But no girl could—no decent girl, that is.'

'I see.' She leaned her head wearily against the cool glass of the passenger window. 'So if I had—strayed, your whole attitude towards me would alter?'

'I see no point in this discussion,' he said stiffly. 'I'm perfectly well aware that you've done nothing of the kind. You don't imagine that things would have proceeded this far between us, if I'd ever imagined . . . oh, hell and damnation, darling, you know what I'm trying to say.'

'I think so. You're saying that while I remain untouched by human hand—or feelings, apparently—then I'll continue to live up to your ideal of womanhood. What would you say, I wonder, if I told you you were all wrong about me?

That I'm just as capable of erring off the straight and nar-row path as anyone else? What then?'

He was very still. 'Are you telling me that you've had a —a sexual relationship with another man?' he demanded at last.

She noticed that he did not use the words 'love affair'.

'No, Colin,' she gave a forced smile. 'My argument is purely hypothetical. I'm still, apparently, as you wish me to be.'

'Then what the devil has all this been about?' He gave a short exasperated laugh. 'God, Janna, I don't understand you this evening.'

'No,' she said quietly. 'And to understand all is to forgive all. Isn't that what they say? Colin, are you sure you want our engagement to continue?'

'Oh, my sweet!' He drew her into his arms again, kissing her averted face. 'I love you, you silly girl,' he whispered against her ear. 'And I respect you. Don't despise me for that. The waiting will be worth it, I promise you. I'll make everything so wonderful for you, darling. We'll be so happy. Trust me?'

She wanted to tell him that it was not a question of her trusting him, but the reverse. Instead she allowed him to kiss her, and said goodnight.

But how much did his love really mean? she asked her-self, lying sleepless later that night. Why couldn't he have said that he loved her no matter what she might have done? That the past was meaningless, and that all that mattered was their future together. Could love really operate within the strict limits he seemed to have set?

Rian's face, dark and jeering, seemed to hang before her in the darkness, and she turned over on to her stomach, burying her face in the pillow and shutting the picture of him away from her.

It was thanks to him that this image of herself as a cool, rather frigid young woman had become the accepted one. Terrified at the dark byways into which her emotions had led her, she had clamped down on all that was young and warm and generous within her, subjecting it to the strictest discipline. With Colin, she thought, these restraints could be allowed to disappear in time. In loving him completely, there could be no harm.

It was disturbing to find how readily he accepted her coldness, how swiftly he had categorised her as a 'decent girl' who could not be expected to understand passion's witchcraft. He did not know her at all, she thought bewilderedly, and when he did encounter the reality, might it not offend him? When they were married would he expect and be content with exactly the same cool passivity she had exhibited up to now? Was she going to be forced to carry this self-imposed deception throughout her entire life?

Oh, dear God, no, she thought. That couldn't be all Colin wanted—a dutiful wife, a gracious hostess and an intelligent mother for his children. Surely he wanted all of her—the reality along with the image.

She was almost glad when the weekend passed and school faced her again.

On Monday morning, she stood frowningly in her slip in front of her wardrobe, trying to decide what to wear. It didn't usually cause her such heart-searchings, she thought irritably, and bit her lip as she realised what this implied. With set lips, she seized her oldest skirt and zipped it up. She was furious with herself, aware now why she had hesitated so long. She knew that Rian would be at the school that morning to bring his child for her first day there.

My God, she thought savagely, I really let his cracks about my appearance get to me.

The skirt and the ancient sweater she teamed with it were an act of defiance intended for him alone, which she could not explain to her mother, who clucked reprovingly as Janna sat down at the breakfast table.

'That jumper's only fit for a jumble sale,' she declared.

'What were you thinking of this morning, Janna?'

'I haven't time to change now.' Janna spread a piece of toast with butter and marmalade and bit into it.

'Nonsense,' her mother said energetically. 'I'll go and look something out for you while you're finishing breakfast.'

'No, Mother.' Janna restrained her. 'These things are fine. I—I'm going to let the children paint this afternoon, and you know what a mess they make. Old clothes are safest. I should hate to ruin anything decent.'

Mrs Prentiss looked anything but satisfied, but she subsided.

Janna gulped down her coffee, said goodbye to her mother and set out to walk to school. The mists and rain of the half-term holiday had cleared, and the morning was bright and sharp with frost.

In spite of her inner turmoil, Janna felt a glow of well-being as she turned in through the school gates. No one could be totally depressed on a morning like this, she thought, relishing the pale washed blue of the sky through the delicate tracery of the bare branches of the trees.

Her footsteps faltered slightly when she recognised Rian's car. She hung around in the staff cloakroom, hoping that if she delayed long enough she would avoid a confrontation with him. But she was disappointed. When she eventually emerged just before the assembly bell was due to ring, Vivien was waiting for her in the staffroom.

'Mrs Parsons would like to see you,' she said cheerfully. 'She has your new pupil with her.'

The headmistress's small room was warm with sunlight and the scent from a big vase of chrysanthemums when Janna entered. At her entrance Rian uncoiled himself from one of the two easy chairs that faced Mrs Parsons' desk and stood up. The deliberate act of courtesy was a pin-prick in itself, Janna knew, and she sent him a fulminating glance, uncaring whether Mrs Parsons observed it or not.

But Mrs Parsons was busy with the hundred and one items that occupy a headmistress on the first day back after any length of holiday. In between two phone calls, she managed to introduce Janna to Fleur, who was sitting perched primly on the edge of the other chair, and suggest she took both the child and Mr Tempest along to the classroom to show them round.

This was most unusual, Janna knew. Normally parents were gently discouraged from following their chicks to the classroom, as it was felt the children would settle better in their absence.

True, Fleur did not seem altogether disturbed by the situation, Janna thought as she preceded them rather stiffly along the corridor. She had a charming, gamine face, and slanting dark eyes that observed this new world in which she found herself with interest but without alarm. It was unusual to encounter such self-possession in such a young child, Janna thought.

Rian looked round the room with its groups of tables and chairs, its walls with gay displays of the children's own work painstakingly presented, and attractively set out library corner, with an enigmatic expression. Janna was unable to assess whether he approved or disapproved, and Fleur was equally impassive.

She calmly assented when Janna suggested where she might like to sit, and returned the stares and greetings of the other children quietly, and without any marked enthusiasm.

Janna turned to Rian. 'I'm sure she'll settle in,' she remarked, hideously conscious that her voice sounded forced and artificial and quite unlike her normal tones.

'I've no great worries on that score,' he returned equably. 'She's an adaptable kid. She's had to be.'

'I'm sure she has,' Janna said with more than a touch of acidity, and thanked her stars inwardly when the bell rang.

'I have to take the children to assembly now. Can you find your own way back to the entrance Mr—er—Tempest?'

'Undoubtedly, Miss—er—Prentiss. But I'm not leaving

yet. Mrs Parsons has very kindly invited me to stay for assembly and see what happens.'

Janna nearly choked. This was an unheard-of thing, again. What could Mrs Parsons have been thinking of? she wondered desperately.

She was only too aware of his mocking gaze as she marshalled the children into a line and set them off walking fairly sedately towards the school hall. As she made to follow them, he detained her with a hand on her arm. She gave him an outraged look and tore her arm free.

His grin was pure malice. 'Don't flatter yourself, my sweet. Have you looked in the mirror today? The drab spinster disguise is well nigh perfect. Is it in my honour?'

'I think it's you who flatter yourself,' she said in her most wintry tone, turning to follow the line of children before it disappeared round the corner of the corridor to the hall. 'I dress to please myself—no one else.'

'If your present garb pleases you, then your taste is deplorable.' He began to walk down the corridor beside her. 'Once you caught a man's eye, Janna. Now you'd stick in his throat.'

'I don't have to put up with your insults,' she said angrily, but there was pain too, mingling with the anger.

He gave her an ironic glance as he pushed open the swing doors into the hall to allow her to pass through before him.

'I think you do,' he said silkily.

Fortunately, he did not stand anywhere near her during assembly. From her place at the end of the row of children, she could see Fleur, her vivid little face turning constantly as she assimilated these new surroundings and happenings.

Janna felt an odd constriction in her heart as she studied the child. What kind of a life could it be for her, she wondered, dragged from pillar to post in the wake of a restless spirit like Rian's? And how did she feel about this separation from her mother? From today's showing, Rian seemed to have assumed total responsibility for the little girl. If she hadn't good and sufficient cause to hate him already, then his casual remark about Fleur's adaptability would have been enough, she thought. Any child, but especially one who had apparently spent her earliest years in the war-torn inferno of Vietnam, needed security and stability.

Perhaps Rian intended to provide this now. Maybe this was why he had come home to this small grey market town nestling in the slopes of the Pennines, but was this the right setting for Fleur? Could the little girl be happy in an environment so totally alien to everything she had been used to?

As she returned to the classroom with the children when assembly was over, she glanced round furtively, but Rian was nowhere to be seen. In this topsy-turvy day, it wouldn't have come wholly as a surprise if Mrs Parsons hadn't invited him to sit in on her classes for the rest of the morning, she thought, seething.

Once back in her room, she closed the door on the world and her problems and devoted her mind and energies to the children. While the other children worked and whispered in their groups, she gave Fleur a reading test, discovering that the child had an extensive vocabulary, although her fluency in stringing words together was poor. At the end of the test, she spoke encouragingly to Fleur, telling her she had done well, and added a few words in French. She was rewarded by a flood of eager words in the same language, far too fast for her to follow, as she was laughingly forced to admit. Fleur looked disappointed but resigned, and Janna guessed she must be getting used to this reaction in this cold grey country which was now her home.

Although she was not on playground duty, she kept a wary eye open out of the staffroom window when playtime came to see how the other children reacted to this stranger in their midst. Fleur was engaged in a game of hopscotch with the girls at her work-table, but watching her across the expanse of tarmacadam, Janna got the oddest feeling that although she was joining in the game, Fleur would have been just as happy on her own. She had none of that eager-

ness to be accepted that so often marked newcomers to the
school. She accepted the other children's overtures, but if
they had not been made, she would have been equally un-
concerned, Janna thought, puzzled. Yet it was impossible
to feel sorry for her. She gave an inward sigh, and turned
her attention back to Beth, who had spent a few days in
London during the holiday and was eager to regale her
with the details, including a visit to the Festival Hall.

During the afternoon break, someone remarked how the
first day after the holidays always dragged, but Janna could
not join in the general chorus of agreement. She felt the
day had flown by, after the awkwardness of its beginning.
After the promised painting session, she was glad to have
an excuse to stay behind in the classroom and finish clearing up. Rian Tempest would almost certainly be collecting
his daughter from school, and she wanted to keep out of his
way as much as possible. She was terrified that he would
make some excuse to seek her out. He seemed to have Mrs
Parsons' permission to come and go as he pleased in the
school, she thought crossly. But the only masculine footsteps to pass her door were those of the caretaker, Mr
Reynolds, and when she left the school a quick glance
around assured her that Rian's car was nowhere in sight.
She breathed a quick sigh of relief and hurried home.

Her mother had a neatly laid tea tray waiting for her
in the sitting room, and the house was full of baking smells
and the promise of a casserole. Janna sniffed appreciatively
as she sank down on the sofa and accepted the steaming cup
her mother handed to her.

'Thanks, Mummy.' She pointed with mock-dismay to a
vivid splash of yellow at the side of her skirt, the result of a
piece of short-lived action painting by one of the boys. 'See
what I meant about old clothes?'

Mrs Prentiss' reply was noncommittal as if her thoughts
were elsewhere, and Janna gave her a surprised glance. But
the explanation was soon forthcoming.

Mrs Prentiss set her untasted cup back on the tray and

said quietly, 'You didn't tell me you were getting a new pupil, Janna.'

Janna felt herself flush involuntarily, and kicked herself.

'It—it didn't seem important,' she improvised desperately, but her mother swept that aside with a wave of her hand.

'Not important that it's Rian Tempest's illegitimate child —and a little Eurasian girl at that?' Her voice was full of reproach.

'Who told you that?' Janna was frankly amazed.

'Deirdre Morris. She called round this afternoon. Said that Beth had talked of nothing else last weekend, and was surprised that you hadn't thought it worth mentioning.'

'I see,' Janna said grimly. She was only too well acquainted with Beth's mother, an inveterate gossip. And she had not realised that Fleur's family history was so generally known in the staffroom. She'd had the impression from Vivien that Mrs Parsons wanted the whole thing treated in confidence. Now, it seemed, it was among the titbits to be passed on by Carrisford's most indefatigable newshound.

She put her own cup down with a faint feeling of nausea.

'I suppose I might have known that the faintest breath of scandal would bring Mrs Morris sniffing round,' she said coldly.

Mrs Prentiss sighed. 'Nine times out of ten, I would agree with you,' she said. 'But, Janna, even you can't deny that it's the Tempest name involved here, and that's what makes it so—interesting.' She shook her head. 'I'm only glad poor Mrs Tempest isn't still alive to see what her precious nephew has made of his life. She had such a strong sense of family pride, and what was due to it. And the Colonel even more so.'

Janna hesitated. 'Colonel Tempest is dead too,' she said. 'And—and Rian has bought Carrisbeck House, it seems. He's going to settle here.'

Mrs Prentiss digested this further piece of information in silence for a moment.

Eventually, she said, 'Well, it seems to show a blatant

lack of concern for other people's feelings to me. This isn't a big, sophisticated city where one's peccadilloes are viewed with tolerance. It's a small old-fashioned place—yes, a backwater if you like, where people still care about things like morality. I know you thought the Tempests were stuffy, Janna, although heaven knows they were always very kind to you, but the fact remains they were held in very great esteem here, and Rian's behaviour will be viewed by many people as an insult to their memory.'

'Oh, Mother!' Janna leaned back against the cushions and closed her eyes. 'For a start, no one really knows whether Fleur is illegitimate or not, except possibly Mrs Parsons, and I know that she hasn't told Beth or her mother. I don't even know.'

'Rian has frankly admitted it,' her mother said with some bitterness. 'Apparently Beth met him in the market square the day before she went to London, and was asking him about the little girl. Then she asked him when he would be bringing his wife to Carrisford.'

'Beth would,' Janna muttered.

'That's as may be. Rian, if you please, replied that he was unable to do so, because he wasn't married and never had been.'

An unwilling laugh broke from Janna. 'I'd give something to have seen her face,' she said. 'Is it too much to hope that her mother was with her at the time?'

'Don't be flippant,' her mother said tartly. 'My sympathy, of course, is for that innocent child.'

'I think you're wasting it,' Janna told her ruefully. 'She seems incredibly self-sufficient—bright, too. In terms of age, she really ought not to be in my class at all, but I know she won't have any trouble in keeping up with them.' She glanced at her mother and saw she was wearing that preoccupied look again. 'You're not listening to a word I'm saying, are you?'

Her mother started visibly. 'I'm sorry, dear. I was just thinking, that's all.'

'About what? You look very solemn.'

Her mother gave her a clear-eyed look. 'That I'm very glad you're safely engaged to Colin. I'm not blind, Janna. I knew all about that crush you had on Rian years ago. I was so worried for you, and never more thankful than when he went away as he did.'

Janna sat very still. 'And yet you never said anything—until now,' she said slowly.

'I never knew quite what to say,' her mother admitted. 'I was afraid that we might quarrel about it, and that I might drive you away. Girls of that age are so strange and touchy sometimes. Then it all seemed to resolve itself, and you suddenly became so much more mature, so I felt I didn't need to mention it after that.' She paused. 'After Deirdre had gone this afternoon, I realised how unsettled you had been this week—all that talk about doubts, and I felt so frightened. Don't do anything foolish, Janna, I beg of you. He—he's too old for you. He was old the day he was born, I think. And deep.' She shook her head. 'People like him alarm me. I want you to be happy, dear, and know peace. The Rian Tempests of this world thrive on conflict and upheaval. He couldn't do that job of his otherwise.'

Janna gave her a long, quiet look. 'I never realised you disliked him so much,' she said wryly.

Mrs Prentiss sighed again. 'I don't dislike him, Janna. I've told you—he frightens me. I can't feel at ease with him. I was never at ease all that summer when he was home for the last time. I was so anxious for you, although your father always said that he would never overstep the mark. It was such a relief when he went away like that. I can't help thinking of this other poor girl—the mother of his baby—and thinking that it might have been you.'

Janna shook her head gently. 'No, Mother,' she said. 'That would have been quite impossible.'

Her mother drew a quick, relieved breath. 'I'm so glad,' she said simply. 'It—it isn't easy to bring up a daughter, as you'll find out one day. There are so many times that you want to pry and you daren't, because you have to respect her privacy. But I can tell you this now, Janna. I'm thankful that you can go to Colin with your head high and nothing to reproach yourself with.'

Janna got to her feet, very pale but with a spot of colour burning in each cheek. 'Colin is equally thankful,' she said. 'You and he seem to think alike on a lot of points. But I don't share your satisfaction, I'm afraid. I may not have slept with Rian Tempest, but I have plenty to reproach myself with just the same—perhaps the very fact that I didn't sleep with him, for one thing.'

'Janna!' Mrs Prentiss looked up at her, appalled. 'You don't know what you're saying.'

Janna shrugged as she turned to the door. 'If it comforts you to think that, Mother, then do so. It seems to make plenty of sense to me. Excuse me now, please. I have some marking to do before tea.'

Safely in her room, she sank limply down on to her bed, staring with unseeing eyes at the cheerful flowered pattern on the wallpaper. So her mother had known about her pursuit of Rian, and had secretly agonised over it.

Perhaps, after all, she could have told her mother about that night at the party and its aftermath, and not had to carry its burden in solitary guilt all these years. Her mother might have understood—then. Yet Janna had deliberately lied to Colonel and Mrs Tempest mainly to protect her mother from the heartache of finding out about her wanton behaviour. Now it seemed as if that tragic lie had all been to no purpose.

She gave a long trembling sigh, and ran her fingers through her hair tangling it. She had protected no one, she thought bitterly. All she had done was delay the day of reckoning for seven years. But there would be no escape for her a second time.

CHAPTER FIVE

THERE was snow on the surrounding hills at the end of the second week, and the first wave of winter coughs and colds had hit the school, exacerbated by the damp chill of the weather.

Janna was not surprised to find that Fleur was among the first crop of casualties. The child had bones like a bird's, and was underweight, though not drastically so, for her age. When a week passed, and Fleur had still not returned to school, she became concerned, particularly as most of the invalids had returned, most of them carrying bottles of medicine and plastic spoons. Janna was adept at administering doses of the various syrups, and resigned that her classroom often had the smell and appearance of a dispensary.

She was using one wet lunch hour to change the wall-display, when Mrs Parsons came in. After helping her fix the remaining section of the frieze and commenting favourably on the work that had gone into it, the headmistress came to the point.

'Mr Tempest has phoned me to say that the doctor won't allow Fleur back to school for at least another week,' she announced. 'He says the child is fretting because she feels she will fall behind in her work, and I was wondering if you could take some work round for her to do.'

It was the most normal of requests, and as the seconds ticked past and she stood immobile, Janna knew that Mrs Parsons was watching her in increasing perplexity.

'Is there some problem?' she asked at last, her brows raised.

Janna moistened her lips. 'None at all. I—I'd be happy to take some books round for her. Is she—are they staying at the White Hart still?'

Mrs Parsons looked even more astonished. 'Mr Tempest
has moved into Carrisbeck House. I thought you knew that.'

Janna's sense of shock deepened. 'No, I had no idea.
That's very quick, isn't it? I thought there would be all
sorts of preliminaries to go through—contracts to sign.'

Mrs Parsons shrugged. 'Presumably all this has been dealt
with,' she commented indifferently. 'In any case, it isn't
really any of our business. So, if you could work out something for Fleur—not too arduous, of course—I'd be grateful. Apparently she has some sort of chest weakness. I'm
afraid she may find this winter very trying until she becomes
acclimatised.'

Janna had by no means finished her display, but when
Mrs Parsons had departed, she swept the remaining items
back into their folder and sat down at her desk. She was so
accustomed to preparing home lessons for children who
were to be absent for any length of time that this request
should not have come as any great surprise. It was part of
her job, she told herself insistently, and she could not avoid
it simply because it would mean her being forced to make
contact once again with Rian Tempest. She had taken such
care to keep out of his way up to now, making minor
alterations each day in the time she arrived at the school,
and left in the evening, and it had been wholly successful.
She had neither heard from him, nor set eyes on him,
although she knew from casual gossip in the staffroom that
he brought Fleur to school each day and fetched her in the
evenings.

There were times when she had even felt optimistically
that perhaps he would never follow up his threats. Maybe he
felt that his mere presence in Carrrisford, and his occupa-
tion of the house that had been intended as her future home,
were punishment enough.

But now she felt that she had been too hopeful, and even
an innocent occurrence like a child's illness was part of the
web in which she was inextricably entangled.

She got up with a deep sigh, and began to look out some

books for Fleur, slipping a set of work sheets into a gaily coloured folder with the child's name on it, and adding some simple puzzles and crosswords of her own devising as light relief.

In spite of the fact that she had a genuine reason for being there, her heart was thumping as she walked up the drive towards Carrisbeck House after school that day. There were some lights on in the house to combat the fast-gathering darkness outside, and Janna thought with a pang, as she had always thought, what a gracious old house it was and what a welcoming appearance it presented. But she must stop herself thinking along those lines, she told herself wistfully. The house was not for her, and she was deluding herself if she imagined it had a welcome for her.

After a momentary hesitation, she rang the bell. She would have given a great deal merely to dump the books she had brought on the step and leave, but she had also brought a load of get-well cards that the children had made for Fleur and she knew that any such action on her part would be inexcusable.

The front door swung open and Rian stood, looking down at her.

'Can I help you?' His brows rose interrogatively—as if she was trying to sell him something at the door, she thought furiously.

She looked back at him defiantly. 'I would like to see Fleur, if I may.'

'Of course.' He stood back so that she could precede him into the hall. 'I hadn't realised that the school provided quite so speedy a service. You didn't have to rush round here immediately, you know.'

She shrugged. 'It won't help Fleur's convalescence if she's bored. I would do the same for any child.'

'What dedication,' he said sarcastically. 'Do you mind if I don't come up with you? I'm making soup and it's reached a rather critical stage. Fleur is in my old room. I'm sure you can remember your way.'

He turned away and Janna began to climb the stairs alone. Stripped of the dark red Turkey carpet she remembered, they had a forlorn look. In fact the whole house seemed forlorn with its bare floors and windows and unshaded lightbulbs.

She had to summon up all her courage to enter the bedroom. Somehow, foolishly, she had expected it to look just the same. But of course, it was now as sparsely furnished as the rest of the house. There was a small single divan bed, where Fleur lay propped up by pillows, a chest of drawers, a wooden chair painted white, and a small twisted pile rug beside the bed, and that was all. No concessions had been made to the fact that this was a little girl's room at all, Janna thought, staring around her. She walked over to the bed with an encouraging smile and drew up the chair.

She thought privately that Fleur still did not look as if she was on the mend. Her cheeks were flushed in contrast to the rather sallow tinge inhabiting the rest of her skin, and her small face seemed to have shrunk.

But she smiled broadly at Janna, and gave her a thin hot hand to shake, as well as politely wishing her good afternoon. She listened with apparent interest as Janna told her what was going on at school, and the plans that were being made for the Christmas concert, but at the same time Janna had an uneasy feeling that the child's close attention was being dictated by an innate courtesy rather than any real enthusiasm. But she did seem genuinely delighted with the cards the children had made for her, and clapped her hands as Janna arranged them on top of the chest of drawers where she could see them.

She did not react as almost any one of her English classmates would have done either when Janna produced the books and work folder from her bag. Janna was used to groans, and sighs of 'Oh, Miss!' and dismayed grimaces, but Fleur's face remained impassive, and she thanked her teacher politely for all the trouble she had taken.

Janna felt curiously defeated as she rose to take her leave.

She had hoped to be able to slip away unnoticed, but Rian was waiting in the hall as she came downstairs, she saw with a stab of apprehension.

He threw open the drawing room door, and stood waiting for her.

'I've made some coffee,' he said abruptly.

'Thank you, but no.' Janna stood her ground.

'Oh, don't be a fool. You've got quite a walk ahead of you, and it's damned cold outside. I'd drive you back, only I can't leave Fleur. She hates to be in bed, and I have to watch her like a hawk.'

'She seems very docile.' With obvious reluctance Janna walked forward and went past into the drawing room. It was furnished solely with a small battered-looking card table and a few folding chairs normally reserved for garden use. A pair of elderly curtains barely met across the french windows.

'As with most young females, the docility is merely a façade. But I don't have to tell you that, do I?' he said smoothly, handing her a large pottery beaker filled with coffee. She would have liked to have thrown it at him, but she was too conscious of the fact of the house's isolation, and that she was alone with him, except for the sick child upstairs.

'Thank you,' she said with an effort, and took a tentative sip. It was very hot, and surprisingly good.

'Yes, I can make coffee.' Apparently he could also read thoughts, Janna thought, flushing slightly as she set down the beaker on the table. 'My soup is highly recommended as well. Can I offer you some?'

'That's hardly likely, is it?' she said bitingly.

'I thought you might have accepted for Fleur's sake. She must get damned lonely here, and some female company would have been a novelty for her. However, I quite understand that even your dedication has its limits.'

'In any other circumstances, I would be happy to stay and have supper with Fleur,' she told him coldly. 'I wouldn't have thought you would be short of female company in any case.'

'Tut tut,' he said mockingly. 'Beware, little cat, your claws are showing. But you don't have to worry. I'm leading an entirely monastic existence at the moment. I'm too busy for anything else.'

She glanced round the room, her lip curling slightly. 'Doing housework, I suppose.'

'No.' She could tell from his tone that her attempt at needling had caused him only amusement. 'I'm engaged on some conversion work at the moment. I'm turning the old stable block into living accommodation.'

Janna's jaw dropped. 'But that's what . . .' she began, and then bit back the remaining words.

Rian surveyed her satirically. 'Go on, my sweet. You were about to say that's what your future father-in-law was intending to do. I'm quite aware of that, although I suspect that our concept of what this accommodation should consist of would differ.'

'But surely you can't just take matters into your own hands like this?' she cried. 'The house may belong to you, but you still need planning permission.'

He drank some coffee, grinning at her over the top of the beaker.

'Thinking of reporting me to your father like a good citizen?' he enquired. 'Don't waste your time, Janna. My uncle was the first person to think of the idea, and he obtained planning permission for the work years ago. It still exists. I made sure of that before one brick was moved.'

She shrugged. 'It's none of my business,' she said stiltedly.

'Since when did that stop a woman from interfering?' he said lazily. 'You forget, you know, when you're away, how ready the tongues are to wag in a place like this.'

'I wonder you came back.'

'No, you don't, Janna,' he said softly. 'You always knew I'd be back, and you know why as well.'

'Just to give the tongues something else to wag about,' she said bitterly.

'That's almost inevitable,' he said drily. 'I know quite well that every move I make is being closely monitored.'

'Well, you have no one else but yourself to blame,' she burst out heatedly. 'Boasting to Beth Morris that you weren't married—flaunting Fleur's illegitimacy in people's faces. Can you wonder if your affairs are suddenly a matter of public interest?'

His attention seemed suddenly arrested as if he had been startled by what she had said. Then he relaxed and gave a faint grin.

'Be sure your sins will find you out,' he remarked. 'Yet what else could I have said to her? She was so obviously bursting with eagerness to be scandalised.' He gave a short laugh. 'I must have succeeded better than I knew.'

'Well, it's too late now.' She drank the cooling remainder of her coffee and stood up. 'Perhaps next time you might stop and consider the effect your thoughtless words might have on innocent people.'

She was thinking of Fleur as she spoke and was unprepared for his reaction.

'Whom did you have in mind?' he asked harshly. 'Your family—or your fiancé's sensibilities?'

She stared at him. 'I didn't mean that,' she began numbly, but he cut across her halting words.

'Last time you pleaded for yourself. Because that didn't work, you're now trying to shelter behind other people. But it won't work, Janna. People are bound to be hurt over this, and there's nothing you can do to prevent it. As you so justly remarked to me a few moments ago, you have no one but yourself to blame.'

She swallowed, fighting a sudden feeling of nausea. For a time there, he had seemed so much more human. Now he had reverted again to being her evil demon—the man who had the power to ruin her life whenever he chose.

He too had risen to his feet and she realised that he was between her and the door.

'Let me go,' she whispered, fighting her rising panic.

He stood, his hands resting lightly on his hips, surveying her mockingly.

'What are you afraid of?' he asked. 'That I'm going to exact my vengeance here and now?' His smile widened. 'You've nothing to fear at the moment. I'm sleeping on a camp bed which only just bears my weight. I'm certain it couldn't cope with two of us, and the thought of an un-carpeted floor cools even my ardour. So you're quite safe —for the time being.'

She could only stare at him, her face white, her heart beating slowly and erratically.

'Oh, don't look so startled, sweet witch,' he drawled. 'You must have known—that woman's instinct must have told you that part of the price you would have to pay me would be the completion of our—er—unfinished business of seven years ago.'

With a speed born of desperation, she was past him and at the door. The knob slipped under her fingers, wet with perspiration, and then the door was open and she was in the hall.

But Rian was beside her, moving without apparent hurry.

'How about this on account?' he said. She was pinned remorselessly against him, and his dark face swam in front of her eyes as his mouth descended.

When at last he raised his head, his breathing was as ragged as her own and little devils danced in his eyes.

'To hell with waiting,' he said unevenly. 'I want you, Janna, and I want you now.'

Her mind was crying 'no' even as her body, deaf to all but its own clamourings, yielded against him. In spite of herself, her arms slid up around his neck, and her eyes closed while her mouth invited his possession.

Then, at first so faintly that she thought it was her imagination, and then more strongly, she heard the fright-ened wail of a child, followed by a small voice crying des-perately, 'Ri-an! Ri-an!'

'Fleur!' His voice sounded like a groan. For a few brief seconds before he let her go, he held her head between the strength of his hands and stared down into her face as if he was memorising her every feature. Then he released her and turned to the stairs.

'Is there anything I can do?' Janna hardly recognised her own voice.

'No.' He looked back at her, suddenly an inimical stranger again. 'She's had a coughing attack and made herself sick. It happens. I can attend to her.' He smiled mirthlessly. 'I'd run if I were you—while I still had the chance.'

She stood staring after him as he went on up the stairs and disappeared. For a moment, she thought her sluggish legs would refuse to obey her, then walking jerkily, she got to the front door and tugged it open. The air outside was like a breath of ice, and she shivered as she stepped out into the darkness.

Just for a while—only a few seconds really—she had wondered what would happen if Rian were to find her there, still waiting in the hall, on his return. But that was madness, she told herself vehemently as she began to hurry down the hill, carried into a run by her own momentum on the steep slope. And as she ran, the sound of her heels on the frosty ground and the thunderous beating of her heart seemed to echo back, 'Madness—madness!'

She found Colin was waiting for her when she arrived home.

'You're late,' he greeted her with a trace of tetchiness as she joined him in the sitting room. His eyes went disapprovingly over her, taking in her tumbled hair, and dishevelled appearance. 'Where on earth have you been?'

'One of my children is away from school with a bad chest. I went to take her some work.' Conscience-stricken over those moments when betrayal would have been so fatally easy, she lifted a penitent face for his kiss.

'You've been running,' he said. 'You're quite out of

breath. Honestly, Janna, there are times when you behave like a child yourself.'

She unfastened her coat and hung it over the back of a chair.

'Running is one way we poor pedestrians can keep warm on evenings like this,' she said with assumed lightness.

'But it's hardly dignified,' he answered.

'Does it matter?'

'Not so much at the moment, perhaps, but you do have your future position to think of.' He frowned a little. 'You really ought to have a car. If it's a question of lessons, I'd be more than pleased to pay for them ...'

'That's got nothing to do with it,' she said, her colour heightened. 'As a matter of fact, I have a licence, but I don't need a car at the moment. The distances I travel during the week simply don't warrant it. Besides, I like to walk. I like to run, come to that, and I'll worry about my "position", as you call it, when I have to.'

'Very well,' he said. His tone was stiff and she knew that she had displeased him. She went over to him and slipped her arms round his waist, leaning her cheek against him.

'Don't be cross,' she begged. 'It was such a lovely surprise to find you here, and all you've done is criticise me.'

He sighed and his arms tightened round her a shade abstractedly.

'I'm sorry, Janna. I've had one hell of a day at work—union problems again. No, I won't be staying for supper. Dad wants a full report on this afternoon's meeting with the shop stewards, and I must get back. He asked me to call. He's giving a small dinner party next Tuesday—four or five people plus ourselves, and he would like you to act as his hostess. Will you, darling?' He smiled down at her. 'It will be good practice for you, you know.'

'And practice makes perfect, doesn't it?' she smiled back at him, wincing inside a little. Colin's attitude that she had to be coached into handling these formal occasions was sometimes irksome, and she could see his father's prompting in all this. 'Am I just to be there to look decorative, or does your father wish me to choose the food and wine and organise the flowers?'

'Certainly not.' Colin sounded faintly shocked. 'Mrs Masham will do all that as usual. You just concentrate on being your own beautiful self, and I'll pick you up around seven.' He kissed her swiftly. 'Bless you, sweetness. Now I must be getting along.'

'Don't go.' She stood on tiptoe and kissed his cheek. 'The report can wait, can't it? You've told me often enough that you're in charge at the works now—that your father is simply a figurehead. Can't you tell him that you're handling this problem, whatever it is, by yourself?'

He gave rather a strained laugh. 'I'd like to hear Dad's reaction if I told him that! You simply have no idea of what's involved, have you, darling? We could have a full-scale strike on our hands if we're not careful. Dad has years more experience of handling these sort of negotiations than I have.'

Janna could have said more, but she decided it was wisest to keep her own counsel. Travers Engineering had a poor record in labour relations over the years, and it was openly said that Sir Robert's intransigent attitude was largely responsible for this. Janna was well aware that it was hoped locally that now Colin was in charge, the works might benefit from a more liberal approach to top management, but it seemed only too likely that Sir Robert's finger was still firmly in the pie.

She took Colin to the front door and waved goodbye to him, then went slowly kitchenwards. For once, her father was home ahead of her, seated at the kitchen table with his pipe going comfortably and the evening paper spread out in front of him. Mrs Prentiss was busy at the cooker, but she turned with a welcoming smile as Janna came in.

'Supper won't be long, dear. Have you had a good day?'

'Fair.' Janna dropped into a chair on the opposite side of the table and smiled at them both. From childhood this had always been one of her favourite rooms, with its gleaming yellow tiles, and shining formica work surfaces. She ran her fingers lightly over the pitted surface of the big wooden table which occupied pride of place. She had made her first attempts at baking at this table, and later pored over her homework there, enjoying the busy flow of the household around her.

Now, if ever, she thought suddenly, was the time to tell her parents the truth about Rian, to confess everything and beg for their help and understanding. She glanced across at her father, frowning darkly over something he had just read, and her mother's untroubled countenance as she adjusted heat levels and peered under the lids of saucepans, and her courage failed her. While there was still a chance that she could prevent them from knowing, then she would keep silent.

She cleared her throat. 'I—I had to take some work round to one of my pupils.'

'Yes.' Janna saw a slight shadow cross her mother's face. 'To the little Fleur child. Beth told me.'

'Beth was here?' Janna stared in amazement. 'Surely not just to tell you that?'

'Oh, no,' Mrs Prentiss denied vehemently. 'Poor Deirdre is laid up with bronchitis so she can't go to tomorrow night's meeting. Beth came round with the minutes book for her. She just—mentioned in passing where you were.'

'How good of her,' Janna said rather drily. Beth was a colleague, but they had never been close. There was a strain of malice in the older girl that had always caused Janna to hold her at arms' length. She had often felt that Beth was aware of this and resented it.

Mr Prentiss folded his paper and laid it down. 'So you've been up to Carrisbeck? Did Rian show you the plans for his stable conversion?'

'No.' Please, dear God, let her not blush. Her mother was watching her closely. 'He—he did mention it, of course.'

Mrs Prentiss sniffed. 'Well, Rian was always a law unto

himself, even as a boy, but I cannot understand why he's bought a lovely house like that if all he means to live in is an old stable.'

'It all depends, of course,' said her husband, 'exactly what plans he has for the house.' He sat back with a faint grin while his womenfolk regarded him.

'You know something.' Mrs Prentiss accused, pausing in the act of dishing-up. 'Is it in confidence, or can you tell us?'

'Nothing confidential about it. He's written to the planning committee putting all his cards on the table, and he's been talking to the *Advertiser* as well, I understand. He wants to turn the place into an adventure centre. You know,' he added impatiently when his wife looked puzzled, 'Outward Bound—that sort of thing. Canoeing on the river, and fell-walking, orienteering and rock-climbing. I can see his point. It's the ideal place for it.'

'But is there a demand for that sort of thing?' Mrs Prentiss persisted. 'I can't think of anyone round this way who'd be very interested.'

Mr Prentiss laughed. 'It's not specifically for local people, Audrey. There'll be parties of young people coming from schools and youth clubs all over the country, I daresay. If he gets permission to do it, that is. I can't see a lot of objection at district level, but if it goes to the County he could have a battle on his hands. With all due respect, Janna, I can't see Colin's father having a lot of time for the scheme. And wasn't he after Carrisbeck himself?'

Janna roused herself with an effort. Her father's news had stunned her. It was in many ways the last sort of thing she would have thought Rian to have been interested in. How little she knew, or had ever known, about him, she thought. She had forgotten too, until her father had reminded her, that Sir Robert was the powerful chairman of the County planning committee.

'Yes,' she admitted quietly. 'He was going to buy it for Colin and me—for us to live in when we were married.'

Her father gave her a dry look over the top of his glasses.

'I think it could prove to have a more useful existence under its present owner. You didn't want to live in that great barn, did you, chicken?'

'What a thing to say!' Mrs Prentiss brought the serving dishes to the table. 'It's a lovely house.'

'Which would cost a fortune to heat and run these days,' her husband completed for her. 'Colin and Janna don't want to start off with a millstone like that round their necks.'

'You talk as if Colin was just some ordinary lad,' Mrs Prentiss protested, as she cut into the steak and kidney pie, and laid neat portions on the waiting plates. 'He has a position to maintain, and he can afford to do it.'

'Colin draws his salary like anyone else at Travers Engineering,' said Mr Prentiss, helping himself to potatoes. 'It's his father who has the real money and Janna and Colin don't intend to live out of his pocket, I trust.' He cocked an eye at Janna who smiled uncomfortably and shook her head. She did not want to admit to her parents that she was pretty sure that was precisely what Colin had in mind. She had often tried to find out from him exactly what their financial position would be when they were married, but he was curiously reticent on the subject, preferring to insist on her giving up her job rather than providing any facts and figures himself. Even the car he drove, she had discovered fairly recently, belonged to the company and not to him. Colin himself seemed to regard the situation as normal, so she told herself that she had no reason to be concerned if he was satisfied. Now her father's words had struck some depressingly familiar chords.

She ate her supper, lending a rather absent ear to her parents' conversation. She would have to talk to Colin again, she thought, and find out precisely how much they would have to live on. It occurred to her that next Tuesday's dinner party could be an ideal time to do some probing. Perhaps she could get Mrs Masham on one side and find out just how much it cost to stage one of those intimate but lavish dinners which Sir Robert regarded as the norm in hospitality. She would need some figures to arm herself with when she talked to Colin. She would have to find out, for one thing, if she was expected to do all the entertaining for Travers Engineering out of her ordinary housekeeping allowance, or whether some kind of expense account would be provided. Otherwise, she thought, the bowls of hothouse flowers and the out-of-season foods that regularly appeared at his father's parties would be entirely beyond their reach, and she doubted whether Colin would be prepared to accept any lowering of standards.

It came to her later that night, as she lay in bed, that in many ways all Colin's standards were impossibly high, and on that note of vague dissatisfaction she fell asleep.

Janna dressed with especial care on the night of Sir Robert's dinner party. She had washed her hair as soon as she got home from school, and blown it dry so that it curved smoothly round her face. She was wearing a floor-length skirt in deep red velvet, teamed with a black jersey top with a scooped neckline. An antique garnet pendant, a legacy from her grandmother, nestled in the curve of her throat.

She looked in the mirror at the smooth, self-contained stranger with the tense mouth and eyes, and gave her a tentative smile. Suddenly a much younger Janna peeped back at her, shy and mischievously appealing. She permitted herself the luxury of a regretful sigh before she turned away to pick up her wrap from the bed.

Colin's car was just drawing up at the gate as she went downstairs. He smiled at her with warm approval as she opened the door to him, and she basked in his regard.

'Lovely Janna.' He kissed her with care, mindful of her make-up. 'A little pale, however. Are you nervous?'

'Not at all,' she replied untruthfully, knowing that it was what he wanted to hear.

She was very quiet as they drove to Thornwood Hall, but Colin did not appear to notice, chatting with obvious satisfaction about his progress with the unions at the works, and the success of the hard line he was taking. Janna murmured a brief response at the appropriate moment, and noticed with faint amusement that Colin never asked her how her day had gone. She was accustomed by now to his attitude that her teaching was just a temporary aberration on the journey from girlhood to wifehood, and could not be viewed in terms of being a career. She sometimes wondered what he would do if she told him she had changed her mind, and would not be leaving her job when they married. He had always taken this completely for granted, but Janna could recall no discussion they had ever had on the subject. Colin simply assumed that she felt as he did about it.

The car turned into the driveway of the Hall, and came to rest on the broad gravelled sweep in front of the house. Colin helped her out, and they walked into the house together. Janna glanced perfunctorily into the dining room as they went past. Everything was perfect as usual—well-polished silver shining on gleaming damask, and candles waiting to be lit in tall holders.

Sir Robert was standing with his back to the drawing room fire when they entered, a glass of his favourite sherry to hand. He gave Janna an all-encompassing stare, then nodded briskly.

As she sat down on the edge of one of the ornate sofas, and accepted the glass he handed to her with some ceremony, Janna reflected not for the first time that this was a lovely room spoiled by over-decoration and fussy furnishings. Only Sir Robert, she thought resignedly, would have considered the gracious lines of an Adam fireplace improved by assembling on it a collection of the most expensive ornaments he could find, arranged without taste, as if they were huddling together for warmth.

She found to her relief that she had met all the guests before. Tonight at least, there were no business rivals to charm, she thought, glancing round with satisfaction and noting that Mrs Masham was hovering in the hall awaiting the signal to serve dinner.

Sir Robert detained her sharply. 'Not yet, lass. We're still one short. Where the devil has the fellow got to?'

Almost before he had finished speaking, the front door bell pealed loudly, and Mrs Masham disappeared to answer it. Janna set down her glass, and rose, smiling, to greet the late arrival. She halted, the blood drained from her face with shock, as she recognised the tall figure in the doorway, devastatingly elegant in his dark dinner jacket and ruffled shirt.

'Good evening, Janna.' Rian took her nerveless hand and raised it to his lips with exaggerated courtliness. 'What an unexpected pleasure.'

'For whom?' she said between her teeth. As she led him across to her future father-in-law, her brain was whirling. Whatever had prompted Sir Robert to invite him? she thought desperately. He could not still be hoping to persuade him to re-sell Carrisbeck House. And why had neither Colin nor his father mentioned to her that he was to be among the guests? She had to acknowledge, to be fair, that she had never asked exactly who was to be there. She knew roughly the circles in which Sir Robert moved, and those that he aspired to, and guessed that the guest list would contain a sprinkling from both.

'Of course you know my future daughter-in-law?' Sir Robert said expansively.

'We're old friends,' Rian returned smoothly. 'An acquaintance I look forward to furthering.'

'Hold hard, young man!' Sir Robert's laugh was slightly uneasy. 'You'll have my lad to reckon with if you're not careful. What do you say, Janna?'

Her face ached with the effort to smile. 'I think Rian is simply being provocative,' she said carefully.

Rian smiled. 'A bad habit,' he said softly. 'I wonder where I could have acquired it.'

She was aware that Sir Robert was eyeing them both sharply, and was never more thankful that it was now time for them to go into the dining room. But her ordeal was only just beginning. It was plain that Rian was in some sense the guest of honour, and he was placed beside her at the table. She unfolded her table napkin with numb fingers. How was she going to get through the evening? She toyed with the idea of pleading indisposition, feigning a sudden illness, but she was uneasily aware that Sir Robert's suspicions might already have been aroused. Her speedy exit might only serve to confirm that she and Rian were better acquainted than she had previously led Sir Robert to believe.

She writhed under the memory of the way Rian had looked at her, the deliberately intimate tone of his voice. His behaviour could not have been more blatant if she had been his mistress of many years' standing, she thought despairingly.

The clear soup was delicious, but it could have been as bitter as gall as far as Janna was concerned. Her features schooled to an expression of polite interest, she joined in the utterly superficial conversations going on around her, hardly aware of what was being discussed.

It was a ploy that served her well through the fish course, but as the plates were being changed and the main course—fillet of beef baked in a light pastry case—was being served, Rian's voice said, soft with amusement, 'You are supposed to talk to me as well, you know. Sir Robert has been glaring at you for fully five minutes.'

She looked at him mutely, her eyes imploring.

'Relax,' he advised drily. 'I don't intend to regale them with your past transgressions over the port, so you can enjoy your meal.'

'Why did you come here?' she whispered.

'Because I was invited,' he answered with a slight shrug. 'Home-made soup can pall, you know. Besides, Sir Robert is so obviously set on making me an offer for Carrisbeck that it seems only fair to give him the opportunity to do so.'

'But have you any intention of selling it to him?'

'None at all, but it provides me with considerable private enjoyment to see him going to all this trouble. The Travers Technique. Snare the victim, ply him with food and wine until he's helpless, and then pounce. It's crude, but I daresay he finds it effective.' He smiled lazily into her eyes. 'Is that the method Colin used when he proposed to you, or did he simply announce a merger?'

'Spare me the witticisms,' she said coldly. 'Colin loves me very much.'

'I hope you're wrong,' he said coolly. 'Otherwise he's going to be very unhappy when I take you from him.'

Her hand moved convulsively, and he covered it with his own.

'Be careful,' he warned softly. 'The captain of industry has his antennae trained on us. Perhaps we should concentrate on this fascinating debate on hunting, across the table, for a while.'

When she finally rose to go the drawing room with the other women, Janna was unhappily aware that she had hardly touched a mouthful of her meal, and that Colin was watching her concerned. She sent him a smile holding a confidence she was far from feeling. Sir Robert's openly speculative gaze she avoided altogether.

She was able to relax a little as she poured coffee, and answer the friendly questions directed at her about her forthcoming marriage. No, she had to confess, they had not fixed an exact date yet, but yes, they were looking for somewhere to live.

'But I thought that was all settled,' Mrs Mortimer, a tall, angular woman with rather carefully styled blonde hair, exclaimed. 'I thought you were going to live here at the Hall.'

Janna set down the coffee pot with extra care. 'Not as far as I know,' she answered quietly, her heart thumping.

'Oh, I'm sure I'm right,' Mrs Mortimer went on. 'Sir

Robert was telling me over dinner that he's been consulting an architect on the matter. He plans to divide the West Wing from the rest of the house and turn it into a self-contained flat for you both.' She gave an artificial laugh. 'Young people today are so spoiled. They have everything made for them, don't they, Jennifer?'

Jennifer Hargreaves, a plump, rather managing woman, who was chairman of the local magistrates' bench, returned her coffee cup to the tray and gave Janna a searching look as she did so.

'Only if what is made happens to be what the young people in question actually want, Alice,' she said dryly. 'I think in this case we may have spoken out of turn.' She gave Janna's hand a brisk pat. 'Don't look so taken aback, my dear. Nothing may come of it, after all, or we may well have misunderstood his intentions.'

She turned to Frances Beckett, the wife of the local master of the hunt.

'I'm a little surprised to see Rian Tempest here tonight, Frankie. I'd heard he was back and in control at Carrisbeck, of course. Do you suppose it means that whatever breach there was has been healed?'

Janna knew Mrs Hargreaves had deliberately changed the subject to be kind and avoid further embarrassment for her, so it was sheer irony that the new topic should be even more unwelcome to her. She bent over the tray to refill Mrs Mortimer's cup, hoping that this action would explain her suddenly heightened colour.

'Breach?' Mrs Mortimer demanded. 'You make it all sound very intriguing, my dear. What happened?'

Mrs Hargreaves shrugged. 'No one knows. On the surface, everything seemed fine, then one day Rian left Carrisbeck House and if you can believe the gossip, the Colonel refused to have his name mentioned in his presence again.'

'I know it was a great sorrow to Agnes Tempest,' Mrs Beckett said slowly. 'We were great friends, and I was very shocked when she told me that they were closing the house and moving to the south. She never hinted at the cause of the quarrel, but she said once she was glad to be going as the house was unbearable to her.' She sighed. 'These family feuds are so distressing. I remember going to a party at Carrisbeck just before all this happened. It was a wonderful evening—Agnes had a positive genius for these things and then within a matter of weeks, the house was closed and the furniture sold.' She turned to Janna with a smile. 'You were there that evening, weren't you, my dear? I remember how pretty you looked and how grown-up. Wasn't it a wonderful evening?'

'Yes.' Janna's face felt wooden. 'It—it was most—enjoyable.'

'As if she remembers!' Mrs Hargreaves exclaimed bracingly. 'My dear Frankie, it was seven years ago, and Janna will have been to hundreds of parties since then.' She gave her a warm smile which Janna was totally incapable of returning.

'Of course, it's obvious what the quarrel must have been about.' Mrs Mortimer, who had been sitting lost in thought, spoke up suddenly. Everyone looked at her. 'Women.' She gave a brisk nod. 'Rian was always very attractive, and there was a lot of talk about his conquests.'

'Indeed there was,' said Mrs Beckett. 'And I'm sure you're right. That would have been anathema to the Colonel, of course. He prided himself on being one of the old school, and he never disguised the fact that he disapproved violently of Rian's whole way of life. I know poor Agnes had to intervene on more than one occasion.'

'There was the Kenton girl,' Mrs Hargreaves said thoughtfully. 'That I do remember. But that wasn't serious. Rian was simply playing the field.'

'And played it once too often,' Mrs Beckett said regretfully. She looked at Janna, her eyebrows lifted. 'You youngsters always knew everything that was going on. Was there a mystery girl in Rian's life, and who was she?'

CHAPTER SIX

THERE was an endless silence. Janna moistened her lips desperately, aware of the curious glances from the older women, but her throat muscles seemed paralysed and would not obey her. And then, as if in answer to an unspoken prayer, the sound of men's voices was heard and the drawing-room door opened to admit the remainder of the party.

Pouring fresh coffee, adding cream, and enduring some rather heavy-handed compliments from the men, Janna was reprieved.

When the coffee was finished, someone suggested bridge. Janna was secretly appalled. She had mastered no more than the rudiments of the game, but all her protests were firmly overruled, and she found herself making an unwilling fourth with Colin and the Becketts.

Sir Robert and Rian did not play. After walking round the tables and bending a benevolently expert eye on everyone's hands, Sir Robert suggested to Rian that they should withdraw to his study, and after a pause Rian quietly assented. As he passed Janna's table, she sent him a long, pleading look. His brows rose and his mouth twisted slightly as he followed in Sir Robert's wake, and she could read nothing from his enigmatic look. Her hands were shaking as the door closed behind them, and she misdealt and had to start again.

It was not a long rubber, although it seemed to Janna to last an eternity. The Becketts won easily, and Janna could see by Colin's compressed lips as he totted up the score that he was not pleased with her performance.

'What's the matter with you, Janna?' he demanded as the Becketts moved out of earshot. 'Some of your bidding tonight was positively half-witted! You'll never learn to play properly, darling, if you don't concentrate.'

She apologised, contritely, knowing that an ability to hold her own at the bridge table was one of the social graces that Colin wanted from her. She enjoyed playing cards, and at one time the task of mastering the intricacies of the game's conventions would have presented an appealing challenge. Now it seemed just another problem to be shouldered.

Colin was going to pour drinks, and with a feeling of defiance she held out her own glass to be refilled. He gave her an astonished look.

'Are you sure you're all right?' he asked in an under-tone. 'You don't usually drink as much as this. You're not nervous, are you?'

'I only want one drink, not the whole bottle,' she said defiantly. 'Poor Colin, am I shattering your illusions?'

'No,' he said tightly. He brought her another drink, his eyes cold with disapproval. 'For goodness' sake be careful, Janna. You had quite a lot of wine at dinner, you know.'

'Yes, I know.' She took the glass and raised it in a mock toast. 'Don't look so worried, Colin. I won't pass out and disgrace you.'

'Such a thought never occurred to me,' he said coldly. 'But please don't let my father see you drinking as much as this. My mother never drank anything stronger than fruit juice.'

'How brave of her,' she said too brightly. 'I'm afraid I shall need something far stronger than that if I'm to face living in the same house with your father.'

A muscle twitched beside his mouth. 'I've never seen you like this before,' he muttered. 'We can't discuss this now. Mrs Mortimer is watching us. For heaven's sake pull yourself together, Janna. You're behaving like a hysterical child.'

'No,' she said. 'You've never seen me behave like that, Colin. For one thing, I tell lies—terrible, damaging lies. And tonight, I feel incredibly truthful.'

His mouth thinned. 'I don't know what you're talking about, Janna, but I advise you to pull yourself together, and quickly too. Dad will be back soon, and I don't want him to see you like this.'

'No, that would never do,' she agreed ironically, and met unmoved his fulminating glance before he turned away.

Janna sipped at her glass, feeling the unfamiliar warmth spreading through her veins. She was beginning to feel lightheaded, she told herself candidly, and deliciously un-caring. For the first time in her life, she could understand why people turned to alcohol when they were in trouble. Recklessly, she downed what was in her glass and walked over to the drinks trolley, ignoring Colin's outraged stare.

As she reached for the decanter, the drawing room door bounced open and Sir Robert stalked into the room. It was evident from merely a casual glance that the genial host had vanished for the evening. In his place was the man who believed in getting his own way, to whom no one said 'no' with impunity, and to whom the impossible had just happened.

Ignoring his guests, he stared fiercely across at Colin.

'Do you know what that damned fool is planning to do?' he demanded furiously. 'He's going to let a pack of bloody kids run wild round the place—and destroy the best stretch of fishing of the river into the bargain!'

There was an awkward silence, then Mrs Beckett rose and diplomatically announced she felt they should be going. Her voice seemed to bring Sir Robert belatedly to his senses, and he made a commendable effort to carry out his duties as host, making his farewells and seeing the guests to the door in a forced imitation of his usual hearty manner.

Janna remained alone in the drawing room. She guessed there was going to be a row, but the prospect was not as dismaying somehow as it would have seemed at the start of the evening. She found she was suppressing a giggle as she picked up the decanter. A hand closed round her wrist and Rian said calmly, 'Don't you think you've had enough?'

'Spoilsport!' She pulled a face at him. 'I'm not frightened of you any more.'

'So I see.' There was a trace of faint amusement in his voice. 'So be it, Janna, if you're determined on your downfall. But you'd better let me pour it. What shall it be—a single or a double?'

'Make it a treble.' She smiled brilliantly at him, and received an appreciative twitch of the lips in return. She wagged a finger at him. 'You're in trouble, you know.'

He laughed. 'There's nothing new in that. But I'm afraid you share his displeasure. As your father is the District Planning Officer, Sir Robert feels you should have given him a hint as to what was in the wind.'

'Oh dear,' she heaved a mock sigh. 'I shall be quite an outcast.'

'An outcast's life isn't so bad. I speak from experience, you understand,' he said ironically. 'The important thing is to make sure you aren't alone in the wilderness.'

His eyes met hers, and Janna felt a sudden dizziness sweep over her that had nothing to do with the amount of alcohol in her bloodstream. A warm sweet quiver of desire pierced her innermost being, and she knew with utter certainty that if he as much as touched her fingertips with his, she would shatter into a million tiny pieces.

She closed her eyes, panic gripping her. This couldn't be happening. She wouldn't let it happen. This was her enemy. He was going to destroy her if he could. If he took her, it would not be solely to satisfy his desire, but also his need for vengeance. As long as she remembered that, she would be safe.

'So there you are.' Sir Robert from the doorway made it sound like an accusation. He came in dabbing a handkerchief at his face, frowning thunderously. 'Funny sense of loyalty you've got, my girl, letting me find out a thing like that from a stranger.' He shot Rian a venomous look.

Janna lifted her chin. 'Why are you so upset?' she asked coolly. 'From what I was told this evening, you no longer

have any real interest in buying the house. You intend that
we shall live here, with you.'

'That doesn't mean I'm in favour of a lot of riff-raff
from the cities coming to stay almost on the doorstep,' Sir
Robert retorted violently. 'It's a mad idea, and I warn you,
young man, you'll have to fight me every step of the way
on this.'

Rian raised his eyebrows languidly. 'I never doubted it,
Sir Robert. Fortunately, you aren't the only member of
the Planning Committee—yet.'

'They do as I tell them,' was the unwise reply. Sir
Robert swung on Janna. 'And you'll do as you're told, too,
so you can just stop looking down your nose, my girl. Having you and Colin here at Thornwood wasn't my original
intention, I'll admit, but it has a lot to recommend it.'

'Oh, it will keep us both under your thumb. I'll grant
you that,' she said tightly.

'Janna!' Colin had followed his father into the room, and
had been standing, silent and uncomfortable, during the
past exchange. But now he interposed himself into the
conversation. 'Where else are we going to live, may I ask?
I've been looking at properties locally. There's nothing
that provides all the amenities we would need. I think it's
extremely generous of Dad ...'

Janna's eyes flashed. 'You outdo each other in generosity,' she exclaimed passionately. 'It never occurred to you
to ask me what I thought of these—unsuitable properties,
of course. And what are these—essential amenities? Does
your wife fit into this category as well—a nice little yes-
girl, who knows her place? Will you put me on the mantel-
piece with the rest of the ornaments?'

Colin appeared to have been turned to stone, but his
father was less inhibited.

'Nice kind of talk, I must say,' he commented virtuously.
'You'll be telling me next that you've joined these Women's
Libbers. Well, tonight's been an eye-opener to me, I can
tell you.'

'And to me.' Janna had already gone beyond the point

of no return, but she was too angry to care. 'I've just found out what it's like to be a chattel. I wonder where I'll figure on the Travers balance sheet—as an asset or a liability?'

'You'll be damned lucky to figure on it at all on this showing!' Sir Robert roared.

'Dad.' Colin spoke pacifically, a hint of desperation in his tone. 'Janna's overwrought. She doesn't know what she's saying . . .'

'Overwrought?' his father echoed derisively. 'Overwrought with my best wines and brandy! I'm not blind or soft in the head either.' He wagged that portion of his anatomy with some vigour as if to prove his point.

There was a soft knock on the drawing room door and Mrs Masham appeared, her eyes rather startled as she surveyed the tense group.

'I beg your pardon, sir,' she began diffidently. 'But the works have been on the phone. Mr Fitzgerald said would I tell Mr Colin that there are pickets at both gates, and they're stopping the night shift going in.'

Sir Robert swore obscenely and swung on Colin. 'I thought you said the situation was under control? Do I have to do every bloody thing myself?'

'But I thought it was sorted out.' For an instant, Janna thought curiously, Colin had looked like a smacked child.

'Well, it isn't. Order the car, Mrs Masham, please and ring the works and say we're on our way.' Personal problems dismissed as the trivialities they were, Sir Robert was obviously relishing the thought of the combat ahead.

'Janna?' Colin said helplessly. 'I—I'm needed, you see. Can I get you a taxi?'

'No need.' Rian rose in a leisurely manner from the large armchair beside the fire where he had ensconced himself. 'I'll drive Miss Prentiss home.'

Colin bit his lip, obviously indecisive, not relishing the suggested solution.

'No!' Janna spoke sharply. 'I'd rather get a taxi—please!'

'You need a lesson in manners, young woman,' said Sir Robert, but his tone was absent, and contained little of its earlier menace. 'Accept the lift when it's offered and be thankful. Can't you see we're busy enough as it is, without trying to get taxis out here at this time of night, charging their fancy prices.'

Janna stared at him for a moment in total disbelief, then she left the room to fetch her wrap. When she came back downstairs, Rian was waiting for her in the hall. He smiled sardonically up at her.

'The techniques of union bashing are being hammered out in there,' he commented, nodding towards the closed drawing room door. 'I don't think we'll be missed if we quietly slip away.'

'I'm not coming with you,' she informed him defiantly, ignoring her swimming head, and the legs that seemed curiously reluctant to obey her. 'I'd rather walk back to Carrisford in my bare feet than ride with you.'

He raised his eyebrows. 'Would you now?' he drawled. Before she could guess his intention, he reached for her swinging her up into his arms like a child. She kicked at him furiously, thinking he intended to carry her, but the next moment she was set down again forcibly, and Rian was casually slipping her shoes into his pocket.

'Let's see how you make out,' he said smoothly, and walked out of the front door and down the steps to where his car was parked.

For a moment, she was so angry that she could neither move, nor speak, nor think. Then she ran after him, tripping slightly on the folds of her long skirt. The stone steps were like ice through her flimsy tights, but they seemed positively pleasurable compared to the gravel she was confronted with when she reached the drive. Rian was in his car, the engine quietly ticking over, watching her, she knew, waiting for her to signal defeat. She lifted her chin. She would see him in hell first, she thought wildly, and stepped out, trying not to wince.

By the time she reached the end of the drive, her tights were in shreds. But that was not her only problem. It was becoming increasingly difficult to walk straight, she had discovered hazily. She tried to imagine there was a white line painted on the road for her to walk along, but the line began to do alarming things, like forming curves and strange intricate patterns, and sometimes dissolving altogether, so she decided to abandon it.

'Pooh to you,' she told it haughtily.

'Oh, my God,' Rian said resignedly. She had been so intent on what she was doing she had not noticed his car drive slowly past and stop a little way ahead. Nor had she observed him get out of the car and walk back to her.

'I'm quite all right,' she informed him, and felt herself sag helplessly as his arms enfolded her. 'Oh, Rian, I feel so ill,' she whimpered against his chest.

'I'm not surprised.' There was a laugh in his voice. 'Dutch courage has to be paid for, my sweet.'

Janna paid. She paid kneeling by the side of the road while Rian held her head, and wiped her face when the spasm was over with his handkerchief. She had never felt so ashamed or humiliated before—except once, and she tried, stumblingly, to tell him so, but he did not seem concerned.

'Everyone's entitled to behave badly once in a while.' He sounded almost soothing.

'But I never behave badly.' She stared up into the frosty starlit sky which, thank heavens, had stopped revolving with the earth at last. 'I haven't behaved badly for seven years. I thought if I tried hard—if I was good then perhaps what I did wouldn't matter so much. But it does ...' Her voice was stopped by tears.

He gave a small harsh sigh, and helped her to her feet.

'I can't wipe out the past for you, Janna,' he said abruptly. 'Not even if I wanted to. Now I'll take you home.'

'Oh, no!' Her hands gripped the lapels of his coat with alarmed urgency. She stared up at him, her face wet, her mouth trembling. 'I—I can't go home yet, Rian. Not like this.'

He muttered an expletive under his breath. 'Hiding behind me again, Janna?' he asked. 'That too has its price.'

'Please,' she whispered. 'I—I can't let my parents see me like this. I'm too ashamed.'

He tugged her shoes from his pocket, and knelt to fit them rather roughly on to her feet. Then he rose and looked at her. 'On your own head be it,' he warned, and turned away.

She followed him tiredly to the car. She still felt nauseated, and her feet were very painful, but that meant little compared with the ache of desolation inside her. Suddenly he had become a stranger again, dark and remote. Yet for a time there, his arms had seemed a refuge rather than a menace. It was too hard for her to understand, she thought, pressing a hand against her throbbing temples.

She sat in silence beside him as he drove, the white ribbon of road unfolding endlessly before them. She did not even ask where they were going. The nausea had passed now, and she felt desperately weary as if a ton weight was pressing down on her eyelids. It wouldn't matter, she thought, if she closed them for a few minutes . . . only a few minutes.

At some time in the future, she was dimly aware that the car had stopped, and that the night air was cold about her. She stumbled slightly. Drowsily she saw lights—a building of some kind, heard Rian talking to someone, the rustle of money, the chink of a key. Someone was carrying her. She was glad about that, because she did not think she could have moved a step unaided. She supposed it must be her father.

But when she opened her eyes, it was Rian, and there was the softness of a mattress underneath her, and the comforting freshness of clean sheets.

'You're not my father,' she said sleepily. 'What are you doing in my room?'

'A good question,' he said rather grimly. 'Perhaps I'll have found an answer by the morning. Now go back to sleep.'

As she began to drift, she felt something brush her hair. For one strange floating moment, she thought he had kissed her, and her last coherent thought told her she was being quite ridiculous before sleep claimed her again.

It was a strange buzzing noise that woke her. For a moment she lay drowsily, then, with her gradual assimilation of the unfamiliarity of her surroundings—the stark white ceiling with the white plastic shade round the bulb, the colourwashed walls, the strident pattern of the cotton bed-spread—she came hurriedly to her senses and sat up.

Rian was standing at the wash basin in the corner, stripped to the waist, using an electric razor. As if he could sense her eyes on him, he turned slightly and she snatched the bedclothes up around her shoulders.

Her startled gaze took in other things. The other bed a few feet away with its rumpled pillow and covers. Her velvet skirt and top lying on a chair in casual intimacy with Rian's dinner jacket and shirt.

'So you're awake,' he said coolly. 'There should be some coffee arriving in a moment. How's your head?'

His casual attitude shook her almost more than the situation in which she found herself.

'Are you out of your mind?' she asked tensely. 'What—what are we doing here? What does all this mean?'

He gave her a long, considering look, then turned back to his shaving.

'We're at the motel at Bartley,' he said expressionlessly. 'You didn't want to go home because you'd had too much to drink and were sick and ashamed. I'd had a hell of a day one way or another and I was too damned tired to drive you about all night, which was presumably what you wanted. This,' he waved a careless arm round the room, 'seemed a reasonable compromise.'

'Reasonable?' She heard the note of hysteria in her voice, and tried to control it. 'Is that really what you think? You've brought me to this place, kept me here all night. How am I going to face my family?'

He switched off the razor and unplugged it. 'Oh, I'm sure you'll think of something, with your inventive mind.'

Janna shut her eyes and lay back against the pillows. Surely this was all a nightmare and soon she would wake in her own room at home, she thought desperately.

'As for keeping you here all night,' his voice went on levelly, 'I didn't notice any protests when we arrived, virginal or otherwise, as the receptionist will no doubt bear out if you ask her.' He put the razor back in its case, and tossed it on to the other bed. Then he came to her side and stood looking down at her.

'Grow up, Janna,' he advised quietly. 'If you're in this trouble, you only have yourself to blame.'

'That's it, isn't it?' she said dully. 'That's why I'm here—like this. Just to satisfy your need for revenge. You've won, Rian. Does it make you happy?'

'My God!' She flinched at the note of suppressed violence in his voice. Then he laughed, and there was something in his laughter that was in some strange way more frightening than his anger had been.

'How right you are,' he said, his lips twisted cynically. 'But it was rather a muted revenge, you must admit, darling. It wasn't exactly my intention that you should sleep through it. But you're awake now, so maybe I should make the most of my opportunity while it exists.'

She tried to twist away, to roll across the bed to the floor, but he guessed her intention and was too quick for her. She was pinned to the bed by hands that hurt, and the mouth that ravished hers was that of a man driven by darker forces than simple desire.

She struggled feebly against the steely arms that confined her, and a soft moan rose in her throat, but he did not relax his grip even momentarily. His kisses plundered the smooth line of her throat and shoulders, and then searched lower, as he ruthlessly dragged aside the sheltering bedclothes.

'What's wrong?' he demanded harshly, his eyes glittering as she tried unavailingly to shield herself with her hands. 'Why this sudden urge for modesty? I've seen you in less, for God's sake, and by your own volition too.'

'I didn't know what I was doing.' She stared into his eyes, desperately seeking a trace of reassurance. But they were like granite.

'Oh, sure. You were just an innocent child, and I was a brutal molester. But that was a long time ago. You may still be innocent, my sweet, but when I've done with you, you won't be a child any longer.'

'Rian!' The plea in her voice was lost in the storm of his kiss. She would not plead again, she thought achingly. She would endure without a word whatever he inflicted on her. She would be ice in his arms.

Almost as if he could read her mind, his mouth gentled on hers suddenly. His hands moved on her softly and seductively in slow tantalising caresses that always stopped short of actual demand. She knew, of course, what he was doing. He was using all his skill as a lover to wear down her defences, to melt the ice barrier she had set up against him. And she also knew, with a sense of burning shame, that it would only be a matter of time before he coaxed the response he wanted from her body.

At long last he lifted his head and looked down at her. There was a stillness between them—an almost unbearable tension, and she heard him breathe her name. He bent over her, and his lips parted hers with devastating simplicity. It was a long kiss. It was a promise and a demand, an offering and an acceptance, peace and turmoil, question and answer. Her arms went slowly up to hold him, and she knew the warm intoxication of his skin against hers.

The sudden hammering on the door was an intrusion almost painful in its intensity. Rian gave a muffled groan and rolled away from her, staring at the door.

'What is it?' he called.

'Your coffee, sir.' They heard the thud and the chink of china as the tray was deposited, and the sound of re-treating footsteps.

Rian sighed and swung his legs to the floor. He sent her an ironic glance.

'Your guardian angel seems to be putting in a lot of overtime,' he muttered as he walked to the door, and re-leased the catch.

Janna watched him mutely while he poured the coffee, and added milk to her cup. He drank his own black, with-out sugar, she noticed. When he had finished, he set the cup on the tray and got up, reaching for his shirt.

'Can you be ready in about ten minutes?' He glanced almost indifferently at his watch. 'It's still very early. We might just be able to smuggle you home without anyone being any the wiser.'

She stared at him, unable to relate this stranger to the lover who had almost drawn her soul from her body only minutes before. Then sudden humiliation flooded her. So this had simply been a diverting interlude, a confirmation of the fact that she was his for the taking whenever he chose to exert himself. She was terribly afraid that she was going to burst into tears, and that would be disastrous.

Her chin went up and her voice was cool as she said, 'Thank you. May I have some privacy while I dress?'

His hands stilled on his shirt buttons, and he sent her a coldly sardonic look. 'What did you imagine?' he asked impatiently. 'That I was going to sit and watch you like some middle-aged *voyeur* in a strip joint? Thanks, but no, thanks. I don't need that kind of second-hand stimulation.'

He picked his car keys up from the table beside the bed and pushed them into his pocket, then grabbed up his jacket and slung it across his shoulder.

'Come down to reception when you're ready,' he told her. 'I'm going to get some petrol.'

The hot water was tepid, but she managed a perfunctory wash before donning her skirt and top. She felt horribly self-conscious as she walked along the corridor and took the lift to the ground floor, and was thankful that no one else seemed to be stirring, except for the staff, who were presumably used to seeing guests in evening dress prowling round the corridors in the early light of day. It was a realisation that brought her no comfort whatsoever.

Rian had apparently completed any remaining formalities, and no one made any attempt to detain her as she walked out through the glass swing doors into the cold grey light. Rian was sitting in the car staring straight ahead through the windscreen. As she approached, he got out abruptly and came round to open the passenger door for her. His face was quite impassive and he did not speak.

The road home lay through wild high moorland country and under any other circumstances, Janna would have gloried in its bleak beauty. Now she sat quietly, staring unseeingly at the road ahead, conscious of nothing but the man at her side, urging on his powerful car with a skill that just stopped short of recklessness.

There was little other traffic on the road, and they made good time. When at last they saw the grey huddle of Carrisford below them in the dale, she broke the silence. 'What are we going to say?'

'Tell what tale you please,' he said briefly. 'Say the car broke down. That's an old favourite.'

'Or I could tell them the truth,' she said hesitantly.

'I don't suppose you even know what that is,' he said bitingly.

She bent her head, smarting at the hurt his words had inflicted. She had intended it to be an overture, an inference that she was now prepared to shoulder the blame for everything that had happened not just now, but seven years ago. His rejection puzzled her. What did he want? she wondered achingly.

The drive through the town was something of an ordeal.

The streets were empty except for a few milk floats, but she felt that every window was a censorious eye watching their swift progress. Her nerves were raw when the car eventually turned into the road where she lived. Everything was quiet, but there was no mistaking the highly-polished blue car parked outside the front gate of her house.

'It's Colin,' she said stupidly.

He gave her a sharp look. 'What do you want me to do? Drive round the block?'

'There's no point. He'll have seen the car.' She wondered bewilderedly why she did not feel more concern. Colin presumably knew that she had not been home all night; that was why he was waiting there. He was going to be very angry, and all she could feel was a kind of tired indifference. Rian braked, bringing the car to a smooth halt beside the pavement. She saw Colin get out of his car and stand waiting for them, his hands on his hips. He had changed out of his evening dress, she noticed, amazed by her eye for such trivial details at a time of crisis, and was wearing a crumpled-looking lounge suit.

Rian came round to the passenger side and held the door open for her. He helped her out, and she knew a desperate impulse to cling to his hand. Instead she squared her shoulders and walked forward to meet Colin.

'Have you been waiting long?' she asked.

'What kind of a question is that?' he rasped. 'Where the hell have you been?' His hand gripped her arm bruisingly. 'Answer me, damn you!'

'That's enough.' Rian took a warning step forward, and Colin turned on him viciously.

'I haven't even started yet,' he said. 'Your turn will come. But for now keep out it. I'm speaking to—my fiancée.' He stared at her. 'Well?'

'When I left the Hall last night I didn't feel very well,' she said evenly. 'I didn't want to go home, and I suppose I must have passed out. Rian took me to the motel at Bartley and looked after me.'

'I'll bet he did!' Colin's laugh had an ugly sound. 'It's all of a piece, isn't it? His own family disowned him, you know, because he couldn't keep his hands off the local girls.'

'That's not true,' Janna burst out.

Colin glanced at her, and his eyes narrowed in unpleasant speculation. 'How would you know?' he inquired. 'You were a kid when all this was going on—weren't you?'

Her eyes fell. She knew she ought to say something, but the words would not come.

'Or was he a cradle-snatcher too?' Colin sneered. 'My God, what a fool I've been! I laughed at Dad tonight when he said you were more than just old acquaintances. I didn't even suspect when you'd gone to his hotel room.'

'There's nothing to suspect,' Rian broke in decisively. 'Take my word for it ...'

'Your word?' Colin glared at him. 'I wouldn't take your word for what day of the week it was!'

'Nevertheless,' Rian went on, apparently unruffled, 'you have no reason to level any sort of accusation at Janna. She is not my mistress and never has been. Now I suggest you take her indoors, otherwise we'll be attracting some unwelcome attention out here.'

'And you wouldn't care for that, of course,' Colin said venomously. 'There's enough unwelcome attention coming in your direction these days. There are a lot of decent people in this town and they'd like to know when you're going to give your child a name.'

'Colin!' Janna was appalled. 'You—it's none of our business. We have no right ...' She broke off in sheer embarrassment, but Rian was smiling, apparently unmoved.

'It's a fair question,' he said. 'Perhaps I'll get round to doing something about answering it one of these days.' He looked at Janna, his eyes dark and enigmatic. 'Goodbye, Janna. In case I don't get another opportunity, I wish you joy.'

She wanted to scream that he couldn't go like this, but she was afraid of setting Colin's hostility into a blaze again. Rian waited for a moment, then raising his hand in a mocking salute, he turned away, climbed into his car and drove off.

'Good riddance,' Colin said vindictively. He stretched. 'God, I could do with some coffee, and a shave.'

'Then you'd better go home,' Janna said quietly. She eased her engagement ring over her knuckle and held it out to him. 'Take this with you.'

He stared at her, obviously taken aback. 'But I don't understand——' he began.

'No?' she smiled faintly. 'I suppose I was meant to feel gratified that you took his word for it that—nothing had happened between us. What were you going to do about last night, Colin? Draw a veil over it and pretend it didn't exist—until you needed a stick to beat me with? I don't think that's what I want in a relationship.'

'You're not yourself,' he said. He took her hand and gazed anxiously at her. 'I'm—I'm sorry, Janna. Is that what you want me to say? But what would any man have thought?'

'Exactly what you did, I daresay,' she said, lifting her hand wearily to push back a strand of hair that the cold breeze had displaced. 'And you were quite right, in a way. It's true I don't—belong to Rian in that way, but it's not because I wasn't—willing. He just didn't—take advantage of me, that's all. Comical, isn't it?'

Colin's face was suffused with blood. He snatched the ring from her hand and stuffed it into his pocket with a furious gesture.

'You slut,' he said hoarsely.

He drove off with a squeal of tyres, leaving a haze of exhaust fumes hanging in the air. Janna watched him go with a feeling of complete detachment, then began to walk slowly up the path. She glanced up at the windows of her parents' room, but the curtains were still tightly drawn, and she supposed that by some miracle they had remained undisturbed by the angry voices outside. She let herself into the house and went up to her room, making no particular effort at quietness, but all was still. She took off the crumpled skirt and let it drop to the floor. Her sweater followed it. She collected a handful of fresh underwear and soaked herself in a hot bath, scrubbing herself methodically from head to foot. She had dressed and was applying her make-up in front of the dressing table before she heard her parents stirring. Her mother came and tapped on the door.

'There you are, darling. You were very late last night. I was quite worried. Did—did everything go well? Colin rang, you know, very late, and I told him you weren't home. He seemed quite upset. You—you haven't quarrelled, have you?'

Janna turned slightly and held out her bare left hand. Her mother put her hand to her throat.

'Oh, Janna,' she said, utterly dismayed. 'What happened? Do you want to tell me?'

Janna hesitated. 'It was no one thing,' she said at last. 'We—we just feel we would be better apart, that's all.'

'I see.' Mrs Prentiss was clearly baffled. She brightened slightly. 'But that isn't really definite, is it? I mean, you could get together again.'

'Oh, Mother!' Janna laid down her hair brush exasperatedly and stared at her. 'It's all as definite as it can be. I never realised my marrying Colin was that important to you.'

Her mother's lip trembled as she sat down on the edge of the bed. 'Is it so unnatural? I—I want the best for you, Janna.'

'And Colin is the best?' Janna gave her an ironic glance. 'I hope I never meet the worst.'

'How can you say such a thing?' Mrs Prentiss looked shocked. 'Up to a few hours ago, you were in love with Colin. Deeply in love.'

'Was I?' Janna sat down beside her mother and considered the matter. 'I don't think so. I was in love with an image I'd created of the sort of man I wanted to love. Colin seemed to—fit that image, that's all. Now I know he doesn't, and I'm glad that I know. You have to love a person, not an image, and we would have been very unhappy if we'd got married.'

'Oh, don't be so silly,' Mrs Prentiss burst out. 'Why, Colin was devoted to you. He would never have given you a moment's anxiety. I don't understand you, Janna, and I never will. You've thrown away the chance of a lifetime, it seems to me, on a whim. I'm not impressed by all this talk of images. I think you and Colin have had a disagreement, and you've acted hastily. Well,' she got up with the air of one who washes her hands of the whole matter, 'you have made your bed and you must lie on it. There's bound to be talk. It's inevitable.'

'I'm sure it is,' Janna said dryly. 'But I'll survive.'

'I expect you will,' her mother retorted bitterly. 'You'll go your own way, as always. But I have to live in this town. I have to listen to the remarks that are made. Plenty of people will be delighted that you and Colin have broken up. He'll have no difficulty in finding someone else.'

'No.' Janna's lips twisted wryly. 'What he wants is a pretty stock pattern.'

Mrs Prentiss' mouth compressed into a thin line. 'I can't talk to you when you're like this,' she declared, turning to the door. 'You've disappointed me, Janna, but I know better than to expect you to give any consideration to *my* feelings!'

She went out, her dressing-gowned figure redolent of disapproval.

Janna watched her go with a sigh. If there was any comfort to be gained from the whole sorry mess, she thought, it was that her mother would never appreciate the true irony of that remark. Then she rolled over on to her side, put her hands over her face and began to weep very softly and passionately.

CHAPTER SEVEN

JANNA felt utterly tired and dispirited when she arrived at school later that morning. Mrs Prentiss had urged her to take the day off, but she had refused. The demands of her job were in many ways exactly what she needed to take her mind off her troubles. And she knew, besides, if she stayed at home, she would be forced to listen to her mother's plaintive recriminations.

Her father had had little to say on the subject. Before he had left for the office he had dropped a light kiss on her hair.

'You know your own mind, Janna. If you have no regrets, then that's good enough for me.'

At the other end of the table, her mother had sniffed loudly.

As she walked to school, Janna had reflected that her mother's reaction had been one of the most disturbing elements in the whole affair, and it threw a whole new light on the relationship between her parents, and their different aspirations. Janna had always known that her father was quite contented to remain in Carrisford, a large pebble in a smallish pond. She had assumed that her mother shared this contentment, and was satisfied with her busy, involved life. Now she wondered whether Mrs Prentiss had merely been using all this activity to mask her disenchantment.

It was clear that it was not so much Colin's personality that had made him an attractive proposition as a son-in-law, but his position, and his father's money, and what that would mean to Janna as his wife. Colin seemed less a person in her eyes than an opportunity—a chance that had been missed. Janna sighed. She felt that a whole new aspect of her mother's personality had been revealed in recent weeks, and one that she did not particularly relish.

And there was also her bitterness towards Rian. Janna found it difficult to comprehend why this had arisen. It was almost as if her mother suspected what had happened, and was in some odd way trying to defend her.

She did not want to think about Rian, she told herself. Such thoughts brought in their train pain and a sense of loss that was well-nigh unbearable. What a fool she had been to think that by closing her mind to him, she could bar him from her heart. Child though she had been in many ways, what she had felt for Rian all those years ago was past all forgetting. She knew that now, and knew too that all that suppressed emotion had merely been lying dormant. Now it was alive again, and a constant torment. She could only be thankful that Rian would never know. What a weapon that would have made for him, she thought sadly.

And yet there had been one wild confused moment on that narrow bed in the motel room when she had thought that he not only recognised her emotion but shared it. That he loved her. She lifted her gloved fingers and pressed them almost unconsciously against her lips as if she was safeguarding the memory of that last kiss.

But that fleeting hope had soon died, she thought. All he had been doing was contemptuously demonstrating his own power. She was no longer his adversary, she was his victim, and how he must despise her for being such easy game.

At least in the classroom she could forget about him, she told herself. And later, as she walked into the room and saw Fleur's small solemn face with the almond-shaped eyes watching her from one of the tables, she realised that, do what she would, she had a constant reminder of him.

For the first time in her teaching career, she wanted to hate a child. But it was a reaction that she rejected with fierce scorn. How could she blame a child for the passion which had resulted in her birth? It was the thought of the mother, that unknown woman who had lain in Rian's arms, that seared her.

She called the register, and accepted absence notes from the convalescents. Fleur, of course, was one of them, and Janna bit her lip as she accepted the envelope. But the writing on it was not Rian's, she was certain. It was definitely a woman's hand. She tore it open and saw with faint surprise that the signature was G. Benson.

She detained Fleur. 'Didn't your—father write this?' she asked, keeping her voice level.

Fleur shook her head. 'My father—away, Mees.'

Janna realised with compunction that she had never given the child a thought the previous night. She had simply assumed that Rian was free to roam the countryside with her until any hour. Surely he couldn't have left Fleur alone in Carrisbeck House with its bare rooms and shadows.

'Then who wrote this?' She held up the note.

Fleur smiled. 'Mees Benson. She kept house for Rian long ago. I stayed at her house last night.' She lowered her voice conspiratorially. 'She is a very good cook, I think. Last night she baked some cakes, and gave me one to eat at playtime. She also gave me one for a friend.' The almond eyes looked unwaveringly into Janna's. 'I would like you to have that cake, Mees. You are my friend.'

'Oh, Fleur,' Janna said rather helplessly. 'She really meant one of the other children, you know.'

Fleur shrugged. 'I want you to have it,' she insisted.

'Very well,' Janna sighed. 'But the others may call you the teacher's pet.'

Fleur lifted a graceful shoulder yet again. 'No matter,' she said, and went back to her seat. Janna placed the notes with the register. She had forgotten all about Mrs Benson, the Tempests' former housekeeper. She remembered now Colin had mentioned the fact that she still kept an eye on the place when they had visited the house that day. Presumably, she still kept an eye on its occupants also. It was

comforting somehow to think that there was a n.
woman to whom Fleur could turn, if necessary.

At breaktime she kept away from the staffroom, awa.
that her ringless hand had already become an item of speculation, particularly by Beth, who had noticed it first. She
called in at Vivien's office and asked if she could see Mrs
Parsons during the lunch hour on a personal matter.

Vivien gave her a surprised glance. 'She's free now, if
you want to see her,' she suggested.

Janna hesitated, then agreed. If she delayed, she thought,
she might well lose her courage.

Mrs Parsons was on the phone again when Janna entered and she signalled her to take a chair while she made
monosyllabic replies to someone at the other end of the
line.

'These mothers!' she said grimly as she replaced the
receiver. 'Terry Wilson's mother wants him to keep his
sweater on as well as his vest for P.E. because he's always
catching cold. I tried to explain that he would catch a
worse cold if we allowed him to do as she asked, but she
wouldn't listen. Now, Janna my dear?'

Janna took a deep breath. 'I'm afraid I have to offer my
resignation.'

'Oh dear!' Mrs Parsons' eyes travelled swiftly to her
left hand and back to her face. She sighed. 'Can I assume
that the fact you're no longer wearing that rather splendid
ring has something to do with this?'

Janna bent her head. 'You could say that,' she con-
ceded. It was odd to recall how only a few short weeks
before she might have been handing in her notice on the
grounds that she was going to be married soon, she thought.

'Oh, Janna.' Mrs Parsons leaned forward earnestly. 'I
know you must be feeling raw, my dear, but don't do anything hasty. Keep your decision in abeyance for a week or
two—you wouldn't be able to leave until the spring anyway. I won't inform the office yet awhile. Who knows,
everything may change, and you may decide to stay with

us. I don't want to lose you, you know.'

'You're very kind.' Janna stared down at her clasped hands. 'But I must leave. I—I know that officially I should stay until Easter, but I was wondering if you would put in a word for me. I—I'd really prefer to leave at Christmas if it could be arranged.'

Mrs Parsons sat back with a slight frown. 'You seem to be very determined,' she commented. 'Are you sure you've thought about this? Teachers' jobs are not easy to come by these days. Have you another post in view?'

'No,' Janna was forced to confess.

'I see.' The headmistress was silent for a moment. 'I won't pretend the office won't consider making a special case. With so many teachers on the dole, they seize every vacancy that occurs. I'll see what I can do. But I hope you're not making a mistake you'll regret. You could be thowing away your training and your security, not to mention your gift with children.'

'It's a risk I'll have to take,' Janna said steadily. 'Everything has been very easy for me so far. From school to college and back to teach in the school I started in. Maybe a little hardship wouldn't come amiss.'

'Hm.' Mrs Parsons was clearly unimpressed. 'I won't phone the office until lunchtime tomorrow. If you change your mind, let me know at once.'

Janna thanked her and left the room. She knew a feeling of relief now that her decision had been taken, and she knew too she would not be contacting Mrs Parsons in the morning. She would be glad to get away, she thought. It seemed the only way she could possibly heal the wounds that the past had dealt her.

She walked back slowly along the corridor. The laughter and boisterous shouting of the children reached her ears quite clearly through the glass of the long row of windows overlooking the playground. On an impulse, she stopped and looked out. There wasn't the slightest doubt that she would miss it all. She liked children, enjoyed handling them and never complained of the noise they made as some members of staff did.

She wondered whether she would seek another teaching job—perhaps even abroad, but somehow it didn't seem to matter much. Just at the moment, she did not wish to consider her future prospects too closely.

The feeling of introspection passed as something on the far side of the playground caught her attention. Fleur was standing there, quite alone, her small body almost pressed against the tall wire-mesh fence which bordered the school grounds. Every line of her tense little figure seemed to spell an almost agonised anticipation. Janna felt disturbed, as she watched her. The child had seemed so content, so well adjusted to her new surroundings. Had they all been too complacent about her?

Janna gave a little worried shake of her head before continuing on her way, resolving she would keep a special eye on Fleur over the next week or so. Everything about at her, at that moment when she thought she was unobserved, seemed to indicate an urgent desire for escape.

It was something they shared at the moment, she thought with a rueful smile as she went back into the classroom. Perhaps, if all else failed, they could run away together somewhere.

She watched Fleur closely for the remainder of the morning, but could find nothing unusual in her behaviour. She was unfailingly polite, and interested, almost disarmingly so. But I'm not disarmed, Janna thought shrewdly. I'm wise to you, young lady, although you may not know it.

At the end of the morning, she introduced the subject of the Nativity play, enjoying the flutter of excitement that went through the room. The days could seem very long for children as November lengthened into December, she thought. Talk of the play and by inference, the end of term, served to bring Christmas that little bit nearer to them. There was the usual rather shy competition among the girls for the privilege of playing the Virgin Mary. All the class beauties fancied themselves in the simple blue robe and white veil wrapped in tissue paper at the bottom of the dressing-up box. But looks, as Janna always swiftly pointed out, were not the main essentials for the performance. An ability to sing a solo rendering of 'Away in a Manger' without forgetting the words, substituting the tune of 'Land of Hope and Glory', bursting into tears or wetting one's knickers with excitement—catastrophes that had befallen some of the previous leading ladies of bygone years—was far more important. Auditions, she said firmly, would start that afternoon.

Before that, however, there was the dinner hour to face. As soon as she went into the staffroom after seeing her class safely into the dining hall, Janna was conscious of that peculiar hush which signals that the subject under discussion has just entered. Her face slightly flushed, she walked over to the trolley where the cups and electric kettle were kept and made herself a cup of coffee. At any other time, she thought, she would have been amused at the stilted and obviously impromptu conversation which had recommenced behind her. She supposed the sensible thing to do would be to take her drink along to her classroom, or even Vivien's office, and let them have their gossip in peace, but she was not in an obliging mood, so she took a chair and made it clear that she was planning to stay.

Inevitably it was Beth who eventually decided to rush in where angels fear to tread.

'You're not wearing your lovely ring, Janna.' Her note of surprise suggested that the observation had just that moment been made. 'Is it being cleaned?'

Janna inwardly applauded her innocent tone.

'No,' she returned coolly. 'Colin and I have simply decided not to get married after all.'

There was an awkward silence, then Beth spoke again.

'What a shame. You always seemed so—well suited.'

'Yes, didn't we?' Janna managed to agree cordially.

'What a blessing that we both discovered in time that we were nothing of the kind.'

Beth was not to be put off, however. 'But won't it make Christmas terribly miserable for you?' she asked. 'You and Colin have always done everything and gone everywhere together. Aren't you afraid that you'll be out in the cold a bit this year?'

Janna's faint smile did not waver. 'I'll just have to keep my fingers crossed that some lonely bachelor takes pity on me,' she said, forcing herself to speak lightly.

There were some sympathetic murmurs at that point from other staff members, and a few hostile glances directed towards Beth, who remained impervious. Her whole attitude, Janna thought, suggested the cat who might not have the cream at the moment, but was shortly expecting a new delivery. It had not slipped her memory that when Colin had first appeared on the Carrisford social scene, it had been Beth who had made the most determined play for him of all the local girls, and she had been openly chagrined at his preference for Janna, who had been the subject of a number of barbed remarks ever since.

She suppressed a slight sigh. There was no doubt that the older girl was ready and more than willing to step into her shoes. Beth would suffer no heart-searchings over Colin's dependence on his father, and would not be deterred at the idea of having to share Thornwood Hall with Sir Robert. In fact, Janna surmised wryly, she would revel in it. Beth knew exactly what she wanted, and would go all out to get it.

She finished her coffee, and with a murmured excuse of having some work to mark, made her escape. She found the atmosphere of rather woolly pity almost harder to take than Beth's overtly malicious attitude. She was not on duty, but the idea of some fresh air seemed appealing, so she collected her coat and went outside. She skirted a group of girls playing an incredibly complex game with rubber balls against the cloakroom wall, and began to walk slowly round the perimeter of the playground. The air was very cold, but fresh, she thought, lifting her face slightly to the wind. She supposed ruefully that from the staffroom she might well look a lonely and tragic figure, brooding over her loss. She could only be thankful that none of the wildest guesses would ever approach the truth of the situation.

Pushing her hands deeper into the pockets of her coat, she had just decided to retrace her steps, when she saw Fleur again, standing at the fence. After a brief hesitation she walked on with a deliberately casual air, and fetched up beside the little girl. Fleur did not jump guiltily, or turn away as many of her contemporaries might have done. She merely turned a calm and somewhat questioning gaze upon her teacher and waited for her to speak.

Janna sighed inwardly and capitulated. 'What are you looking at?' she asked. 'The road doesn't seem very interesting to me.'

'I am waiting for Maman,' the child announced quietly.

Janna's heart gave a swift uncomfortable thud in her chest.

Trying to sound neutral, she said, 'Is that a good idea?'

Fleur nodded. 'Oh yes,' she said calmly. 'She will come very soon now. If I stand here, I will be able to see her as soon as she turns the corner.'

'I see.' Janna was silent for a moment. Then, aware that she was flushing slightly under Fleur's clear glance, she said, 'Who—who told you that your mother was coming? Was it your father?'

'No.' Fleur's shake of the head was a positive one. 'She told me so herself. She has written to me. I think she has also written to Rian, but he did not speak of it.'

'Oh,' Janna said helplessly. She walked on, knowing that Fleur was once again absorbed in her self-appointed task.

The child's revelation that her mother might be coming to Carrisford in the near future was a disturbing one, the implications of which Janna did not care to examine too closely. But in spite of herself, she could not help wondering what Fleur's mother looked like. Did she have that quality of remote beauty that seemed to appeal so strongly to Western men? It seemed more than likely, as there were already traces of it in her daughter. Janna bit her lip savagely as the image of a sweet-faced Oriental beauty rose strongly in her mind. Was whatever attraction there had been between them—and she could not pretend that it had not been a strong one if it had resulted in Fleur's birth—still alive? Or might it not be that this visit to Carrisford could well revive it? She lashed herself with these thoughts as she walked back into the school, deliberately accepting the pain they brought in their wake.

She had to face the fact that Rian might have decided to conciliate convention by a belated marriage. He would have a great deal to gain by it, after all, she thought numbly, not least the certainty of having his daughter with him permanently. She closed her eyes tightly, aware that burning misery was threatening to overwhelm her.

Rian had achieved his desire to make her wretched, she thought wanly, although not in the way he had originally envisaged. Her only consolation was that he would never know of his own success, although she had come near to betraying herself when he had left her that morning. She had been so close to wearing her heart on her sleeve and begging him to stay with her. Only Colin's furious presence, and her fear that they might come to blows, had kept her silent.

Now she was thankful that she had given Rian no hint of the naked longing that consumed her. Nothing had really changed, she told herself drearily. She had no right to Rian. She never had done. She had wanted him, and in return had roused a basically physical response in him. Now there was another woman in his life, presumably able to arouse a similar response, who had a very definite right to his love and respect. If he had now decided to legalise the union between them, and remove the slur of illegitimacy from his daughter, no one could blame him.

During the afternoon, as she had promised, she held the auditions for the Nativity play. The boys were soon dealt with. Few of them wanted to play the speaking parts, and the remainder were quite happy to be shepherds, and Wise Men's attendants and guests at the inn. But there was a queue of little girls wanting to be tested for the part of the Virgin Mary. It was plain that the other feminine roles of the Angel Gabriel and the innkeeper's wife were regarded as pretty poor pickings in contrast.

The only one who hung back was Fleur, but there was an undeniably wistful air about her, Janna noticed as she tuned her guitar. She gave her an encouraging smile.

'Aren't you going to sing for me, Fleur?' she asked.

There was a brief but noticeable hesitation, then Fleur gave a resolute shake of her head. Janna did not press the point at that moment. She had a group of eager children waiting to be heard, and there would always be time to squeeze Fleur in at the end if she changed her mind.

There was a wide variation in the standard of the performers, but the favoured candidate seemed to be Lucy Watson, a dark-haired, blue-eyed charmer, who attended dancing classes in a neighbouring town, giving her a considerable edge over her less poised contemporaries. Lucy knew she was the best. It was inherent in the demure but triumphant wiggle of the hips she gave as she returned to her place amid the vociferous applause of the rest of the class.

Janna supposed the decision had been made for her. It was almost a Watson prerogative, playing the Virgin Mary in the annual Nativity play. Lucy was the youngest from a large family, and Janna could well remember a very much older sister of the said Lucy playing the part when she herself had been a pupil at the school.

Perhaps for this very reason, she delayed making the announcement after the other children had finished singing. Ignoring the expectant hush, she looked slowly round the small group who had declined to try their luck on the grounds of tone deafness or preternatural bashfulness.

'No one else want to try?' She strummed a few soft chords by way of inducement, and her eye caught Fleur's. 'Come along, Fleur,' she said briskly. 'I don't think I've ever heard you sing.'

Slowly and reluctantly the child rose to her feet and came to the front of the room.

'What must I sing?' she asked.

'Do you know "Away in a Manger"?' Janna played the opening bars.

Fleur shook her head, her small face impassive at the tiny ripple of incredulous giggles that went round the room.

'But you've heard the others singing it,' Janna went on persuasively. 'Look, here's a book with the words in it. Just try the first verse. Go as slowly as you like.'

She began to play the familiar tune on the guitar, picking out the notes clearly to guide the child, and after a moment's uncertainty Fleur relaxed her shoulders and began to sing. It was as if a captured bird had suddenly opened its heart in that classroom. Her voice was high, sweet and pure with a quality about it that Lucy Watson could not even aspire to. And her ear was good, Janna thought. She sang the tune that she had heard her classmates sing without faltering once. When she had finished there was a puzzled hush, then a scattering of applause. Lucy was both admired and feared by many in the class.

Janna waited until the wriggling and the whispering had died away.

'It's a very hard choice because you all sang so well this year,' she began diplomatically. 'However, I think Fleur will make a lovely Virgin Mary for us.'

There was a breathless pause, then Lucy Watson, rosy with temper at being baulked of what must have seemed certain victory, put up her hand with bravado.

'It's not fair, Miss,' she said stridently. 'Why, she didn't even know the song without you helping her. Besides, she's foreign-looking.'

There was an awed gasp from some of the girls at this piece of plain speaking, which Janna silenced with a look.

'That will do, Lucy,' she said coolly. 'You have to learn to lose as well as win, you know.' She turned to Fleur, noticing rather anxiously that she had turned very pale. 'Here's the book,' she said, as if it was all an everyday occurrence. 'You can learn the words quite easily. It isn't a very long carol.' She looked at the rest of the class. 'We'll have the first rehearsal tomorrow lunch-time—shepherds and angels only, please.'

The bell rang, and the children crowded to the door, delighted to have a minor sensation to report at home that evening. Janna had put her guitar in its case and locked it into her stock cupboard when she felt a small tug at her sleeve. Looking down, she saw Fleur staring at her, urgency written large on her face.

'Yes, dear?'

She saw with alarm that Fleur's eyes were full of tears, which she was struggling to master.

'Mees—please don't make me do it,' she appealed, a tiny sob in her voice.

'But why not?' Janna sat down at her desk. 'Is it because of what Lucy said? You mustn't take any notice of that, you know. She was just disappointed. She didn't mean ...'

Fleur shook her head. 'It isn't that. It isn't fair for me to practise for this part when I will not be here for the play.'

'But what makes you think you won't be here?' Janna recognised she could be on dangerous ground here.

Fleur looked down at the floor. 'My mother says that when she comes, she will take me away with her.'

Janna bit her lip. 'But you can't be—sure,' she pointed out gently. 'Perhaps when she comes here and sees how nice it is, and how happy you are, she may decide to live here too.'

Fleur shook her head again. 'She will not do that. It is not what my father would want.'

'You can't be sure of that either.' Janna sought for wisdom to say the right thing. 'Maybe he's got used to being —part of a family again.'

Fleur shrugged. 'I do not think so,' she said. 'He does not care about us. He did not care enough to marry my mother when he knew I was to be born. Often she has told me this.'

Janna felt the words like a dagger-thrust. It was hateful being presented with this uncaring portrait of Rian, and not being able to repudiate it. She tried to change the subject.

'It's such a pity to deny the rest of us the chance of hearing you sing,' she tried a different tack. 'You have a lovely voice. Who taught you?'

'My mother.' Fleur's lips trembled perceptibly. 'She is a singer. Her name is Kim San, and one day I will be a singer too.'

'I wouldn't be in the least surprised,' Janna agreed, trying to smile. 'In the meantime, we'll just wait and see what happens, shall we? Perhaps your mother won't come until after the play, and that means you can play the Virgin Mary, and still go and be a singer afterwards.'

She waited and was rewarded with a reluctant nod, and a shy and increasingly delighted smile.

When Fleur had gone, she sat for a long time at her desk staring in front of her, and not liking very much the pictures that her imagination was inexorably painting.

So Fleur's mother was a singer, and if the gift she had passed on to her daughter was anything to go by, a very good one too. She found herself wondering under what circumstances Rian and this Kim San had met. There seemed little doubt that, whatever they might have felt for each other in the past, now there was a great deal

of bitterness in their relationship. She sighed. Fleur was
such an attractive child that it disturbed her to think that
her parents were involving her in their disputes. It was not
fair for such a small girl to be so knowing, and so acceptant
of the things that could go wrong between a man and a
woman.

She wondered if this was part of the pattern of their
relationship, taking the child to live with each of them in
turn, then uprooting her just as she seemed to be settling.
They seemed to be using Fleur as a pawn in some mon-
strous game, and it was little wonder that the child allowed
herself to show so little overt emotion. She had probably
had to learn to hide her feelings.

Janna gave a muffled groan, burying her face in her
hands. In ordinary circumstances, when she came across
a situation like this, she would have to weigh very carefully whether any good would be gained by having a talk
with the parents, or asking Mrs Parsons to do so. But in
this case, she dared not interfere. She felt altogether too
involved, and could not trust herself to take an objective
view of the matter, where her sole concern would be to do
what was best for Fleur.

In her own mind at least, she was certain that the little
girl needed a settled environment for a considerable period
to draw her out of her shell and make her realise her full
potential. But at the same time, she knew that it was impossible for her to suggest this to Rian, feeling as she did.
It would be tantamount to pushing him into the arms of
another woman, she thought unhappily.

Supper that evening was not a particularly comfortable
meal, but Janna was too absorbed in her own thoughts to
notice this overmuch. She registered the fact that her
mother was unusually silent, and given to heaving deep
sighs, and that her father was frowning and pensive.

'You see,' Mrs Prentiss roused herself to say with a
kind of injured triumph when Janna pushed her half-filled
plate to one side, 'you're fretting. You can't deceive your

mother.' She gave Janna a beseeching look. 'Go and phone him, dear. I expect you'll find he was just going to pick the phone up himself. Everyone has these tiffs when they're engaged. You'll look back in twenty years and laugh at all this.'

'Maybe I shall, but it won't be with Colin.' Janna rose to her feet. 'No, I won't have any dessert, thank you, Mummy. I—I think I'll go upstairs and do some work. There's a documentary on television I'd like to watch later on.'

Once in her room, she wandered restlessly between the bed and the window. She wanted something to happen, but she didn't know what. In her heart, and she cursed herself for being a fool, she hoped that Rian would make contact with her in some way, even if it was only to find out what had happened after his departure. Just to hear his voice on the end of a telephone would be something, she thought achingly. She sank down on to the bed with a trembling sigh. She despised herself in many ways. This wanting she felt for Rian was like a fever in her blood. There was nothing rational about it. It belonged to Janna the girl, not Janna the woman she now was. And knowing all she did about him—the way he had treated the girl who mothered his child, even his uncaring behaviour towards that child—she still could not tear him out of her heart. He was too deeply entrenched there. He had been her first love, and she knew now, with a sense of total inevitability, that he would also be her last. If she could not belong to Rian, then she would belong to no one else.

The telephone rang downstairs, and she tensed unbelievingly. Didn't they say that if you concentrated hard enough upon something you wanted, then it would come to you? she thought wildly, and waited for her mother's disapproving voice to call up the stairs to her. But no one called, and she could hear the subdued murmur of conversation below.

She relaxed with a feeling of disappointment so intense

that it was painful. Glancing at her watch, she saw it was almost time for her documentary. She decided she might as well go downstairs and watch it. Brooding in her room waiting for non-existent phone calls was doing her no good at all. As she descended the stairs, her mother replaced the telephone receiver and turned away.

Her eyes met Janna's. 'Deirdre Morris,' she said with a shrug of resignation, and Janna knew, with a dreadful impulse to laugh, that her mother's cup of bitterness was now full to overflowing.

Somewhat to her relief, Mrs Prentiss did not follow her into the sitting room, where her father was seated going through some papers, his briefcase open beside him. He glanced up as she came in. 'Change channels if you want, my dear. I shall be busy with these for a while.'

When her programme was over, Janna was relieved there was no one present asking questions on what she had just seen, because she knew she would be able to answer none of them. She jumped slightly when her father spoke.

'The great man descended on us today, or on me to be precise.'

'Oh, Dad!' Janna felt sudden dread grip the pit of her stomach. 'What did he want?'

Mr Prentiss gave her a quizzical glance. 'Well, he didn't give me the sack, so don't look so worried.' He laughed. 'It would take more than Sir Robert and all his much-vaunted string-pulling to get me off my perch. Although I must say he made it clear he wasn't pleased. Not pleased at all,' he added slowly.

'He—he mentioned Colin and me?'

'Not in so many words. But he talked of rank ingratitude and made a veiled reference to King Cophetua and the Beggarmaid which I could understand or not if I chose. I chose not,' said Mr Prentiss. 'No, what he'd really called about was this scheme for Carrisbeck House. He wants me to advise the committee to send it through to County level for a final decision.'

'Can he do that?' Janna asked doubtfully.

Her father shrugged. 'Dubious, I'd say. It can perfectly well be dealt with at District level. The fact is he wants a finger in this particular pie, and he's willing to use any means at his command to obtain it. He as good as told me he had most of the members of his committee in his pocket. Hinted that he'd take the thing to appeal and beyond, if he had to. Seems very much against it one way or another,' her father said slowly.

'Against the scheme itself, or against Rian?' Janna was bitter, staring into the fire. She did not see the quick glance her father sent her.

'A bit of both, I'd say.'

'Can you understand what he has against it?'

'I think so.' Mr Prentiss began to fill his pipe. 'But as they're mostly founded on personal pique and not good planning reasons, I don't intend to take much notice of them. I gave him to understand as much.'

'Oh, Dad!' Janna gave him a troubled look. 'What did he say?'

'There wasn't a great deal he could say.' Mr Prentiss got his pipe going to his own satisfaction. 'My next appointment was waiting and my secretary had buzzed twice, so he went off breathing threatenings against the world in general.'

'He didn't treat you like that when I was engaged to Colin,' Janna said forlornly.

Her father patted her arm. 'Now don't start thinking like that,' he admonished. 'Your personal life is your own affair, and Sir Robert has no more business than anyone else to drag it into the public sector. He'll get over this broken engagement in time. Probably by tomorrow when he's calmed down he'll be telling everyone what a lucky escape his lad's had.'

His tone was so like Sir Robert's own that it forced an

unwilling laugh from Janna. She leaned back against his chair.

'Will Rian get permission to do what he wants with the house?'

'I don't see why not. There are no firm grounds against it—the house isn't a listed building, and if it's left empty for many more years it could just become a derelict white elephant. And it isn't as if he wants to turn it into a night club, or one of these infernal country clubs. Then we would have to stop him because that road isn't wide enough to accommodate all the extra traffic. But the kids using Carrisbeck aren't likely to arrive driving their own cars and causing a jam back to the market place. I've discussed it with our chairman, and all in all, he thinks it's a fair idea.' He paused and looked at Janna. 'Has that put your mind at rest?'

She started uncomfortably, aware of the implication in his words. 'Heavens, no. Why should it? It's nothing to do with me.'

'Methinks the lady doth protest too much,' Mr Prentiss quoted. He smiled down at Janna, but there was a trace of anxiety in his eyes. 'For someone who is not concerned, you're taking a devil of an interest in the progress of Tempest's affairs.'

'I'm just interested because I knew the house,' Janna mumbled. She jumped to her feet, smoothing out the creases in her skirt. 'It's late, and it's going to be a busy day tomorrow. We start rehearsals for the Nativity play.'

'How the years roll by!' Her father gave a reminiscent grin. 'I suppose there's a Watson playing the Virgin Mary.'

'Not this year.' Janna returned the grin. 'I think you're in for a surprise.'

'Not too great a one, I hope,' Mr Prentiss called after her. 'We don't take kindly to surprises, here in Carrisford.'

They were words that Janna was to remember before too long had passed.

CHAPTER EIGHT

JANNA came out of the school gates and turned towards home with a feeling of thankfulness. She had never felt this before at the end of a school week. She enjoyed teaching, and was never happier than when she was busy and involved in her work, but the last ten days had been oddly disturbing ones, and she could not help but be glad they were over.

She had hardened herself to the fact that her broken engagement and subsequent resignation would be a nine days' wonder when they were generally known, and she had not been disappointed. Fortunately, Mary Bristow, the head of the infants' department, had just discovered that she was going to have a baby, and this had now taken precedence over Janna's affairs as the staff's most absorbing topic of conversation. Nevertheless, she had not had an easy time of it. Most of her colleagues seemed to share her mother's opinion, she discovered, and she'd had to put up with a number of lectures on being adaptable and learning to give and take.

But that was not all. She had expected that, and could cope with it. What she had not bargained for was the subtle alteration that had taken place in her relationship with the children in her class.

She could not have defined it to save her own life, but she knew it was there just the same, and it worried her. Suddenly there was a slyness about some of the children which had never existed before, an attitude that verged on insolence which she had not previously encountered with any of them. And the most worrying thing was that it seemed to have begun just after she had chosen Fleur for the leading part in the Nativity play.

145

Her intuition told her that Lucy Watson was at the bottom of it all, but she had no real grounds for this assumption. Lucy was polite and demure, almost exaggeratedly so, yet once when Janna had found herself unexpectedly at odds with one of the other children, she had observed an odd gleam in Lucy's eye which could have been triumph.

She felt bewildered and distressed. Surely Lucy's influence over her peers was not so great that she could disrupt almost an entire class because she had been disappointed over a part in a play? She tried to tell herself she was imagining things, but she knew that it wasn't so. There was something there, something insidious and unpleasant.

Children who would once have turned cartwheels for her if she had asked them now did the absolute minimum and stared in silence when she took them to task. When she asked for volunteers for small jobs, no one moved. It was, she thought, troubled, rather like being sent to Coventry.

But she was unable to find a motive for their strange behaviour. Children had a strong sense of justice, she thought, and they all knew in their hearts that Fleur was easily the best singer in the class, so why should she feel so sure that it all stemmed from that?

It was beginning to tell on her too. She now snapped where once she would have reasoned, threatened where she would have persuaded.

She sighed, and pulled up her coat collar against the chill wind. Everything was going wrong, she thought drearily. The only certainty was that at the end of term she would be jobless. Mrs Parsons had managed to secure her early release from the education office, and Janna thought that if her relationship with the children was to deteriorate much more, she would be glad to leave. No one could possibly give of their best in such an atmosphere.

Only Fleur herself seemed totally unaware of what was happening. Janna, when she had first realised the change in the children's attitude, had kept a wary eye on her, in case this covert hostility she had sensed might take a more tangible form where Fleur was concerned. But it did not seem to be so, and anyway Fleur's own quality of aloofness made it difficult to gauge exactly what kind of a relationship she had with her schoolmates. If she was being bullied, she gave no sign.

Certainly she spent most of her time in the playground on her own, but Janna was sure this was at her own choice. The child still stood by the fence, staring up the road with undeniable longing, and in spite of her own very mixed feelings, Janna could not help hoping that her mother would come soon. It was pitiful to see the air of expectancy dwindle as she kept her small vigils.

Janna could well comprehend her soreness of heart, she thought wryly. It was a feeling she shared. She had not seen Rian or had any form of communication with him since he had driven away from the house that morning, leaving her with Colin. He was out of sight, and out of reach, and she had to live with the pain of that each day, and take it to bed with her at night. At first, she had nursed the vain hope that he would at least telephone to make sure that she was all right. Then, as the news of her broken engagement became more widely known, she had told herself that he was bound to hear about it.

But if this was true, it only served to underline his total indifference, she thought bitterly. He must have realised that the most telling form of vengeance he could have exacted was to cut her out of his life altogether. The calculated cruelty of it left her numb.

It was one thing to tell herself that she had to do the same—wipe him from her mind as if he had never existed —and another to achieve it. She could not walk down a street without wondering if she was going to come face to face with him. Everywhere she looked seemed to have some association, however tenuous, with him.

And she could not even confide her misery to anyone.

It was naturally assumed that if she was fretting it was for Colin, and that she only had herself to blame.

She could only promise herself over and over again that things would be better when she was away from Carrisford, and pray that it would really be so. She had no idea even where she would go. London did not attract her particularly, but she felt she needed the busy oblivion of a large city to bury herself in for a while. At least there she would not feel she was living out her existence under a microscope.

She squared her shoulders as she walked up the path and into the house. Her mother had still not accepted the situation, and treated her with a mixture of long-suffering and tacit reproach which Janna found wearing on the nerves. Her first diffident mention of the fact that she had given in her notice had induced a migraine attack lasting two days, and Mrs Prentiss had refused to discuss the matter since. This refusal by her mother to face the facts was just one more problem on a rapidly lengthening list.

Summoning a dutiful smile, she walked into the kitchen, where Mrs Prentiss was occupied in getting the evening meal ready. She was bending over the oven when Janna entered, and her face seemed flushed, but whether this was because she was cooking, or caused by temper, Janna could not be sure. But her doubts did not last long. Mrs Prentiss straightened herself, and banged the oven door shut with unnecessary emphasis, and the stare with which she favoured her daughter was openly resentful.

'Is something the matter?' Janna asked mildly. She slid into a chair at the kitchen table, and pulled the teapot and waiting cup towards her. No matter how deeply she might be in her mother's bad books, the ritual of having a warm drink waiting for her when she returned from school never altered.

'Oh, no.' Mrs Prentiss' tone was heavy with irony. 'What could possibly be wrong?' She picked up a paring knife and launched an assault on a bowl of harmless-looking potatoes.

Janna sighed. 'That's what I'm waiting for you to tell me,' she pointed out patiently.

'So she hasn't told you.' Her mother gave a snort of laughter. 'Well, I suppose not even she had the brass face to say anything under the circumstances.'

Janna stirred her tea resignedly. 'Who hasn't?' she persisted. 'And what is it that I should know?'

'Beth Morris, that's who!' Mrs Prentiss filled a saucepan with water and slammed it on to the draining board. 'Her mother took great delight in telling me this afternoon. She's going to the Christmas Ball next week—and your Colin's taking her!'

'No, she didn't mention it,' Janna acknowledged quietly, 'But at least it explains what all the whispering in corners over the past couple of days has been about.'

'You don't even seem surprised.' Her mother rounded on her. 'Don't you care that you've been supplanted?'

Janna sighed. 'Not particularly,' she said honestly. 'And you have to hand it to Beth—she certainly doesn't waste a lot of time.'

'Is that all you can say about it?' Mrs Prentiss cast her eyes to heaven. 'Well, you've lost him now, Janna. Beth Morris may have caught him on the rebound, but she won't let him go in a hurry.'

'Mother,' Janna leaned forward, a note of earnestness in her voice, 'I'm sorry you're upset, and that's all. If Colin and Beth want each other, then I wish them luck.'

'Very generous, I'm sure.' Mrs Prentiss hunted in her overall pocket for a handkerchief and blew her nose vigorously. 'Oh, Janna, with the chances you've had, I never thought I'd see Beth Morris married and you left an old maid.'

Janna forced a smile. 'You seem very sure that will be my fate,' she said with an attempt at lightness.

'I'm sure of one thing.' Mrs Prentiss resumed her attack on the potatoes. 'If you're still hankering after Rian Tempest, you've made a big mistake.' She gave a grim laugh. 'He has other fish to fry.'

Janna sat very still. She wanted to ignore what her mother had just said, to brush it aside, but she could not. If it was more than just a casual remark, she had to know just what was behind it.

'Are you trying to tell me something?' she asked at last.

'So it is him.' Her mother put up a weary hand and pushed her hair back from her forehead. She shot Janna a glance of mingled pity and anger. 'You fool, Janna. You wouldn't be warned. He's not interested in you any more, my dear. Not now that his fancy woman has come back.'

Janna's mouth went dry. 'His ...?' She could not get the words out.

Mrs Prentiss gave a little nod. 'She arrived on the midday bus from Leeds. Deirdre said she had two large suitcases with her, so it's clear that she means to stay. And she took Fred Collins' taxi straight up to Carrisbeck.' She caught sight suddenly of her daughter's white face set in rigid lines, and her mouth puckered. 'Oh, Janna, he's no good for you. He never was. Why didn't you believe me? And after all the trouble I went to ...'

Janna bit her lip. 'It's all right, Mummy.' She tried and almost succeeded to control the tremor in her voice. 'I—I knew she was coming. Fleur did mention it.'

'Poor little mite,' Mrs Prentiss said fiercely. 'I only hope he's prepared to do the right thing by them both at last.'

'Yes,' Janna said. She got up steadily from the table and went out of the room. In the hall, she paused, looking around her as if she had just woken to discover herself in a strange land. She did not know where to turn or which way to go, but if there had been any means of escape, she knew she would have seized it. Yet flight was denied her. Whatever her personal feelings, she had to stay in Carris-ford for another two weeks at least, until the school term ended. Besides, if she ran away as soon as Kim San arrived on the scene, people might draw exactly the kind of conclusions she was most anxious to avoid. She wanted to have at least the remnants of her pride about her when she left.

Somehow, somewhere she would find the strength to get through these last days here, and when she left, she would hold her head high and no one, not even Rian—oh God, especially not Rian—would ever know the agony that was flaying her spirit.

She came down late to breakfast the next morning to find preparations for an early lunch already going on, and her mother flying round the house, dressed to go out except for her topcoat which lay waiting over an adjacent chair.

'Oh, heavens!' Janna sat down at the kitchen table and looked at her ruefully. 'I'd quite forgotten. It's the Christmas Bazaar this afternoon, isn't it?'

'Yes,' her mother agreed. She sent her a sideways look. 'It's all right, dear. I know you said you would help out, but I quite understand if you don't feel up to it. We can manage.'

'No,' Janna gave a resolute shake of her head. 'I—I'd like to help still. I need something to do.'

Mrs Prentiss paused as if she was on the verge of saying something, then with a short sigh she compressed her lips and turned away.

The bazaar, which was invariably held in the large assembly room attached to the town hall, was the largest event of its kind held during the year, and was organised by a committee drawn from all the women's organisations and churches in the town, who shared the proceeds between them. Mrs Prentiss had been a leading light of this committee for a number of years now, and Janna, whenever she was available, usually lent a hand either serving behind a stall or helping with the teas.

It was a popular event attracting visitors from all over the area, and business was brisk from the moment the doors were opened. Janna, who had been sent to help on the Christmas card stall, was kept too busy to give her own problems even a moment's thought, which was what she had hoped.

In spite of the rush, however, she was uneasily aware that something was wrong. The three women who were manning the stall with her were old acquaintances. In fact, they had known her since babyhood, yet their manner could not have been cooler if she had been a complete stranger to them. Janna supposed resignedly that this must be some kind of strange backlash from her broken engagement, but she found their attitude difficult to comprehend. She had not realised that Colin was so popular locally. In fact, with the industrial troubles at Travers Engineering escalating with every day that passed, she might have been forgiven for supposing the opposite to be the case. Sir Robert had carried out what amounted to a lockout, and it looked as if the dispute was going to drag on over the Christmas period.

She gave a little sigh and began to rearrange some of the remaining packets of charity cards.

Mrs Armstrong, who was in charge of the stall, came across to her. 'They're serving tea now, Miss Prentiss. Perhaps you'd like to go and have yours.'

Miss Prentiss—and from someone who had been calling her Janna since she was in her pram. It also occurred to Janna that helpers usually went to have tea in pairs, and it was only too obvious that none of the others wished to accompany her. Her face slightly flushed, she gave a quiet word of agreement and walked towards the side room where the teas were situated.

She glanced round casually as she entered, recognising numerous familiar faces. But as she collected her tray and made her way to a table she had to acknowledge yet again that her reception had been chilly, to say the least.

In a way, she was thankful that the table was an empty one. She was beginning to think she would not know how to cope with yet another snub from normally kindly people who had known her all her life. She sat down and lifted her plate of sandwiches and cakes off the tray, and as she did so she was aware that someone was standing beside her. She glanced up and saw to her astonishment that Colin was standing there, with Beth Morris beside him. Beth looked bright-eyed and attractive, the large fur collar of what was clearly a new coat drawn up around her pointed chin.

'Hello, Janna,' Colin said awkwardly. 'This—this is quite a surprise.'

'Not really,' she said composedly, well aware that there were curious eyes fixed on them from all over the room. 'If you remember, I do help here every year.'

'Oh, yes.' Beth gave an artificial little laugh. 'But this year somehow I think we all felt you might be keeping— what do they call it?—a low profile.'

Janna added sugar to her tea and stirred it. 'I can't think why.'

'No?' Beth began rather shrilly, and Janna, to her astonishment, saw Colin nudge her into silence.

He sent her an uncomfortable look. 'I—I'm sorry about all this, Janna. It can't be very pleasant for you, but I want you to know it was none of my doing. You have—rather— brought this on yourself, you know.'

Impatience rose within Janna. 'I wish I knew what you were talking about,' she returned. 'You didn't used to talk in riddles.'

'No?' Colin's discomfort was becoming more evident with each moment that passed. He sent a look round the room that was positively hunted, then turned away. 'Come on, Beth. I—I think we've spent enough time here.'

'More than enough.' Beth lingered, however, looking down at Janna with an air of unmistakable triumph. 'We have to hurry,' she said. 'Sir Robert hates to be kept waiting, you know.'

Janna gave her an ironic look. 'Dinner at the Hall?' she asked sweetly. 'That's quick work.' She regretted the words as soon as they were uttered, but it was altogether too late.

Beth's eyes gleamed with malice. 'You're a fine one to talk!' she retorted with emphasis. 'But at least I'll be ending the evening in my own bed.'

'What do you mean?' Janna felt as if an icy fist was twisting in the pit of her stomach.

Beth shrugged. 'Ask Mrs Watson,' she returned. 'I'm sure she'll be only too glad to enlighten you. All right, Colin, I'm coming.' She turned on her heel and walked away, leaving Janna fighting hard to gain her composure. She pushed the plate of food away, feeling that another bite would choke her, and got up from the table. Somehow she had to get to the bottom of this. At school, she had been sure that Lucy Watson was responsible in some way for the unpleasant atmosphere. Now it appeared that her mother was generating the hostility she had sensed that afternoon. But why? Simply because Lucy had not been given the role in the play that she coveted? It seemed too trivial to contemplate.

She poured the remains of her tea into an empty cup awaiting collection on a nearby table and walked towards the tea urn where Mrs Watson was stationed. She was a tall handsome woman, in spite of her rapidly greying dark hair, showing clearly where Lucy had derived her good looks from. The glance she gave Janna as she approached was clearly inimical.

'More tea—Miss Prentiss?' The deliberate pause carried a calculated insult.

'Thank you.' Janna held out her cup with an assumption of calm. 'How—how are the family?'

'As well as can be expected.' Mrs Watson splashed tea into the cup and added milk from a large glass jug.

Janna hesitated. 'I'm afraid Lucy was rather disappointed not to get the part of the Virgin Mary in the play at the end of term,' she said, deciding to take the bull by the horns.

'We were all disappointed,' was the cold reply. 'None

more so than our Maureen. She'd set her heart on her little
sister playing the part she'd had. And she was very put
out when she heard who'd been picked instead of our Lucy.
Very put out.'

'I'm sorry you should have taken it like that,' Janna said
quietly. 'But I think when you see the play, you'll have to
agree that Fleur has a very lovely voice and . . .'

'Lovely voice!' There was contempt in Mrs Watson's
tone. 'You're not fooling anyone with that tale, Miss Prentiss, though you may have had a college education and
think you're a cut above the rest of us. Our Maureen never
had a college education. All she could manage was a job
as a chambermaid in a hotel, but at least she's kept herself
respectable.'

Janna felt sick at the venom in the older woman's voice.

'I think I'd better go before you say something you may
regret,' she said quickly, and made to turn away, but Mrs
Watson gripped her arm, oblivious of the fact that people
were watching.

'Would you like to know where she's working now, Miss?
At the Bartley Motel, that's where, and she was on duty
one Tuesday night not so long ago. She saw you arrive, and
she saw you leave—and you engaged to another man.'

Janna was as white as a sheet. Mrs Watson continued
inexorably, 'You don't fool us any more with your airs
and graces. You gave that Fleur child the part in the play
to try and please your fancy man, and a lot of good that's
done you, from what I hear.'

Janna's voice sounded numb and dead in her own ears.
'You're wrong—quite wrong. I didn't . . .'

She was suddenly terribly aware of the listening ears
all around them, picking up every damning word that had
fallen from Mrs Watson's lips; the eager eyes, assimilating
with delighted horror the latest sensation to break in the
little town. She tore herself free from Mrs Watson and
headed for the door, half-blinded with tears.

She was not even aware that there was anyone standing

in the doorway, until she collided with them. Strong hands seized her shoulders as she stumbled, forcing her to remain upright. Her startled eyes looked up to meet Rian's.

'You?' she whispered brokenly. 'Oh, God, Rian, let me go!'

'Don't be such a fool,' he said grimly. 'You're not in a fit state to go anywhere, apparently. Kim, grab that chair over there.'

Dizzily Janna was aware of a subtle, elusive perfume. She glanced up and saw a piquant heart-shaped face with dark almond-shaped eyes, and a soft mouth curved now in a sympathetic smile. In the prosaic interior of the assembly rooms, Kim San was like some exquisitely exotic tropical blossom, strayed by chance into a village horticultural show.

'Please.' She shook her head. 'If I could just have my coat. I must leave. You don't know ...'

'I think I do.' His mouth was set, his face carved in lines of granite. 'But you can't leave alone. I'll drive you home. Kim, you'll be all right?'

Janna's coat, somehow, was around her shoulders and she was being manoeuvred through the crowds to the door.

'But your—Kim,' she gasped, as they reached the exit. 'You can't leave her here like this.'

'Why not?' He gave her an irritated look. 'She won't come to any harm, and all this is a novelty to her, remember.'

'I suppose it would be,' Janna said dully.

She was silent until they were in the car and driving through the market place crowds. Rian's face was taut and unyielding as he manipulated the high-powered vehicle through the teeming streets. Janna leaned back against the smooth leather of the seat, her eyes closed. She felt totally shattered by the scene with Mrs Watson, but at least she knew now the source of the poison which had entered her life, though she might not be able to fight it. A tear squeezed down the curve of her cheek. Beside her, she heard Rian curse softly under his breath. The car came to an abrupt halt. Dazedly she opened her eyes and found that they were parked in a small side-street.

Then Rian's arms were round her, drawing her towards him until she felt the warm steady beat of his heart under her cheek, and she wept against him, a long soundless, mindless outburst of hurt and pain and humiliation, while his hands held her and his voice murmured things she only barely heard.

When she could master her voice sufficiently to speak, she said, 'You—you know what happened?'

'Yes.' He was silent for a moment. 'Janna, as God is my witness, whatever I intended, I didn't mean it all to end like this. I never dreamed ...' He halted abruptly. 'Oh hell,' he said angrily, but whether his anger was directed at her or himself, she could not fathom. His hand came under her chin, forcing her face up to meet his, and he kissed her, her lips, her eyes, her tear-stained cheeks, until the world dwindled to the pressure of his mouth on hers.

Compulsively, her arms fastened round his neck, her fingers tangling in his dark hair, as her slim body arched against his in a silent offering.

'Janna!' He half-groaned her name, then thrust her forcibly away from him. He sat for a few moments, gripping the steering wheel, fighting for his self-control, then he leaned forward and flicked the ignition switch. 'I'll take you home,' he said tonelessly.

The journey was soon accomplished. Janna sat slouched in her seat, staring ahead of her with blank eyes. When the car stopped, she sat up with a jerk, fumbling for the catch on the passenger door.

'Wait,' Rian said impatiently. He got out, and came round the car to open the door. His hand gripped her arm bruisingly as he helped her out of the car, and slammed the door shut behind her. He steered her towards her gate, and she tried to pull away from him.

'Thank you—but I'm all right now.'

'Don't be a fool,' he told her curtly. 'You're not fit to be left on your own.'

'I don't want your pity!' She wrenched her arm free, furiously.

'You're not getting it.' He was still implacably at her shoulder when she reached the front door. Her hand shook as she fitted the key into the lock. The house was empty, she knew. Her mother was still at the bazaar, in happy ignorance of what had transpired, Janna hoped with all her heart, and her father would be at the golf club.

Her voice trembling, she said, 'Rian—please go.'

He put out a hand and stroked her cheek lightly. 'Presently,' he promised.

He pushed her gently but firmly towards the sitting room. 'Go and sit down. I'll make some coffee.'

'But you don't know where everything is,' she protested, conscious of how feeble it sounded.

'I'll manage,' he said briefly. 'Do as you're told.'

She walked into the sitting room, and switched on the tall standard lamp in the corner, then she drew the curtains and took the guard away from the front of the fire, adding more fuel and coaxing it into a blaze.

Rian came in carrying two steaming cups and deposited them on the small table in front of the sofa. She sipped at hers and gasped, 'What's in it?'

'Some brandy. I found a bottle in the pantry.' He gave her a look of faint amusement. 'Have you lost your taste for it?'

She coloured, remembering only too well the last disastrous occasion on which she had drunk brandy.

'I don't think I ever had one,' she said wearily. 'I just needed some—Dutch courage, as you said. Is this why I'm being given a second dose of the medicine?'

'No.' He stretched his long legs out to the fire, and gave her a considering look. 'I think your own courage will carry you through this, Janna, if you'll let it.'

'Thank you for the good advice.' She set the cup back

on the table. 'It must be a great satisfaction to you to know that you've achieved everything you wanted. You wanted to see me—brought low, didn't you? Well, I'm down, Rian. I'm on my knees.'

'I'll have to take your word for it,' he said slowly. 'I never believed your emotions were so involved.'

'No?' she gave a little, bitter laugh. 'It's all right, Rian, you don't have to bother about it. Just write it off as another adolescent crush. Only this time, I've hurt no one but myself. There's a sort of rough justice in that. It should please you.'

He swore violently, setting his own cup down so sharply that half the contents deluged the carpet.

'To hell with justice,' he said furiously. 'I'm not interested in that, and you know it. But is it just a crush, Janna? God help me, but I have to know.'

She shrank into the corner of the sofa, her eyes dilating wildly as he reached for her.

'No, you mustn't ...'

'And who's going to stop me—you?' He shook his head slowly. 'I don't think so, Janna, and this time I intend to make sure.'

His weight crushed her against the softness of the chintz-covered cushions. Eyes closed, she fought him, her mouth clamped tightly shut against the insistence of his, her hands braced against his muscular chest. Then with a rush of shamed urgency, she realised she was fighting no one but herself. There was no sense of triumph in his conquest, but she was aware of passion barely held in check. It would take so little, she knew, for the final barrier between them to be swept away. So little.

When at last he lifted his head, the expression in his eyes both frightened and exalted her.

'Your room,' he whispered unsteadily. 'Where is it?'

For a moment, she was tempted—tempted to snatch what happiness she could while it was being offered. It would only take a word from her and heaven could be hers.

But what kind of hell would take its place ultimately?

A sudden vision of Kim San rose up in front of her, with all her slender, appealing charm. And there was Fleur to think of too. At last Fleur had the chance of a settled home—family life. Rian belonged to them now. They were waiting for him even at this moment.

With a little cry of self-disgust, she pulled away from him. 'You have no right,' she accused him, a break in her voice. 'No right ...'

'No,' he said heavily, at last, 'I see that.' There was a long pause, then he got up and reached for his car coat, draped across the back of the sofa. She watched him dumbly, unable to move or speak.

He fastened the coat, watching her with sombre eyes.

'So it's goodbye, then,' he said quietly. 'I had hoped it might turn out differently. But I suppose it was always impossible. Too much has happened. Too much hurting, too much bitterness.'

'At least no one else will be hurt,' she said tonelessly.

'Oh, no.' His soft mirthless laugh sent a knife twisting in her heart. 'No one at all. Goodbye, sweet witch. I won't ask you to forgive me.'

She stayed motionless where she was, hearing the front door close behind him, and seconds later the sound of the car engine as he drove away.

She looked dully at the coffee cups, telling herself that she should clear them away—find a cloth and mop up the carpet—do a hundred and one useful and meaningless jobs to keep the ache of loss and longing that was beginning to overwhelm her at bay.

Rian had gone, and she had sent him away to Kim—and to Fleur who needed him. And the knowledge that she had behaved well was no consolation at all for the feeling of despair that filled her.

She sat for a long time in the quiet room, dry-eyed, her face buried in her hands while she tried to come to terms with what had happened. She was brought back to the pain of reality by the sound of the front door opening, and her mother's voice calling anxiously to her.

She made herself reply, and a moment later her mother came in, unbuttoning her coat, reaching for the main switch and flooding the room with light.

'Oh, there you are, Janna,' she said in a relieved tone. 'I wondered what had happened to you. Mrs Armstrong said you had gone home early—she thought you had been taken ill perhaps.'

'Is that what she said?' Janna asked dryly.

'Well—not in so many words,' Mrs Prentiss said rather fretfully. 'I can't remember what she did say—but I know it was—odd. But then everyone's been odd this afternoon. People have been passing the strangest remarks.' Her eyes fell on the used cups. 'Has someone been here?'

'Yes,' Janna paused. 'Did—did no one tell you that Rian Tempest brought me home?'

'No, they didn't,' Mrs Prentiss said sharply. 'And it's a wonder, because I've had nothing else but Rian Tempest —Rian Tempest pushed down my throat all afternoon.' She gave Janna a troubled look. 'Was that wise, do you think?'

Janna shrugged. 'Probably not,' she said quietly, 'but it doesn't matter any more. He's gone now, and he won't be coming back.' She moistened her dry lips. 'He—he'll probably be getting married quite soon.'

'She was there with him this afternoon, you know, and the child. People were saying it was brazen.'

'People would.' Janna gave a sigh. 'What else did they expect—that he was going to immure them both at Carrisbeck House?'

'She's quite a pretty thing,' Mrs Prentiss said abruptly. 'Perhaps everything will work out for the best.'

'In this best of all possible worlds.' Janna hid her pain under a mask of irony.

Her mother leaned towards her. 'It will be all right,' she said emphatically. 'Believe me, Janna, he wasn't right for you—a rolling stone—never settled for five minutes, and wanting to drag you round the world in his wake—a child like you.'

She stopped abruptly, two bright spots of colour clearly visible in her cheeks, and her hand crept up slowly to cover her mouth.

'Mother,' Janna stared at her, a feeling of incredulity beginning to steal over her. 'What are you talking about?'

'Nothing.' Mrs Prentiss stood up, reaching for her coat with hands that she tried and failed to keep steady. 'I—I must just hang this up ...'

'Later.' Janna detached the folds of material from her mother's nerveless fingers and motioned to her to sit down. Her voice was very gentle. 'What makes you think Rian ever wanted to take me round the world with him? He never told me so. Did he tell you?'

Mrs Prentiss' mouth was trembling. 'I did it for the best,' she whispered. 'You must believe me, Janna, I did it for the best. You were so young. You couldn't have known what you wanted.'

'What did you do, Mother?' Janna persuaded.

Her mother gave a long, quivering sigh. 'Wait here,' she said tonelessly. She was only gone from the room a few minutes. When she returned, she was holding an envelope. She handed it to Janna, who saw to her amazement that it was addressed to herself. She had never seen Rian's hand-writing, yet she knew instinctively it was from him. She stared at her mother. 'When did this come?' she asked.

'Look at the postmark.'

Janna complied. 'August?' she exclaimed. 'But it's almost December! You've had it nearly five months.'

Mrs Prentiss shook her head. 'Seven years,' she said quietly. 'You were out when it came, so I opened it. You were still a child. I had a right to see who was sending you letters—at least I told myself I had. I—I was afraid it was from him, when I saw the London postmark.'

Janna extracted the single sheet of paper from the en-velope and unfolded it.

It wasn't a very long letter. 'Janna,' it began uncompromisingly, 'I wanted to see you before I left, but it wasn't possible. You must never blame yourself for what happened at the party. There had been trouble brewing between my uncle and myself for some time. You were just the catalyst. I was angry for a while, then I remembered how young you were and how frightened. Anyhow, I can't be angry with you for long. There was another row before I left Carrisbeck. I told my uncle I was going to return in a year's time and marry you. He was furious and said that if I did any such thing, I would never see a penny of his money, or get the house either. Well, sweet witch, will you wait a year for me? I can't promise you much of a life. We may not have a permanent home for some time. It will be hotels and living out of suitcases. The paper is sending me back to Vietnam in two weeks' time. If I haven't heard from you by then, I'll know that you really were too young all the time. Rian.'

Janna lifted her head dazedly and looked at her mother.

'You kept this from me,' she murmured. 'You kept it all this time. But why? I don't understand.'

'Because you were so young—too young to decide whether or not you wanted to go with a man like that. I was afraid for you.'

Janna stared down at the letter again. 'And so he went to Vietnam thinking I didn't want him—that it had all been a schoolgirl's escapade, and he met Kim,' she said in a low voice.

Mrs Prentiss gave an angry sob. 'It didn't take him long to forget about you, and turn to her. You were well rid of him, Janna.'

Janna shook her head, still disbelievingly. 'He never mentioned the letter,' she said, half to herself.

'No.' Mrs Prentiss produced a handkerchief and dabbed convulsively at her eyes and mouth. 'He promised he wouldn't mention it to you. I never meant to either—unless it was some time in the future, when you were safely married to Colin.'

'When did he promise you this?'

Mrs Prentiss looked down at the floor. 'He came here one night—with some library books. You'd left them somewhere and he found them and brought them here. He—he wanted to speak to you then, but I told him that you were happy with Colin. That you'd had a slight tiff, but it was all over and that you would soon be back together again. I said that you were going to be married just after Christmas and live at the Hall.'

'I see,' Janna said numbly.

Her mother bent her head. 'I don't expect you do,' she said. 'One day you'll have a daughter of your own, and then you'll know. It's been so hard all these years, pretending I knew nothing, hoping and praying that he wouldn't turn up. I was so thankful when you met Colin and seemed to be settled. But all *he* had to do was show his face and you were after him.' She gave a sigh of great bitterness. 'But it's over now, isn't it?' she said. 'We can forget about it—can't we, Janna, and start to live our lives again?'

'Yes.' Janna looked at her mother's white, pinched face and forced a little smile. 'It—it's over.'

CHAPTER NINE

FACING her class the following Monday morning was not the easiest thing Janna had done in her life, but at least she knew the worst now, she told herself. She was no longer striking at shadows. She could not believe that Lucy or any of the children knew the whole story, but undoubtedly they believed that she had preferred Fleur to Lucy in order to please her boy-friend, and had thus behaved unfairly.

She was cool and brisk with them all, taking them unhurriedly through the timetable but making sure at the same time that they were all constantly occupied and had no opportunity to hatch any mischief.

By the time a couple of days had passed, her policy had paid off, and the majority of the children were their old selves again. Or maybe they were just tired of Lucy and her self-importance, Janna thought.

Fleur too seemed a different child since Kim San's arrival in Carrisford. Her small face was alight, and she fairly bubbled with excitement and pleasure.

'My mother says we shall stay here and not go away for a long time,' she confided to Janna one break time. 'When the host-el is open, we shall work there and cook food and make beds for all the people who come to walk and climb.'

'And where will you live?' Janna asked. It hurt, but she had to know.

Fleur considered for a moment. 'Rian is making an apartment for us. It will be very nice. There will be a little room for me to sleep in, and a big room where my mother and father will sleep.' A big smile transfigured her face. She lifted it to Janna confidentially. 'They are going to be married—my mother and father. It will happen very soon now.'

'That's wonderful,' Janna forced herself to say. Inwardly she prayed that the ceremony would be delayed until after she had left the area. Mentally, she was counting the days. She had not dared tell her mother that she would not even be spending Christmas in Carrisford. Mrs Prentiss was so patently eager to make amends, and was busily planning all kinds of festivities. It seemed cruel to destroy her hopes, yet it had to be done. Janna had written away to a country hotel offering house parties for single people and had been offered a last-minute cancellation which she had thankfully accepted. When the holiday period was over, she would see what she could do about finding herself a job, trying Liverpool or Manchester first, she had decided.

She had not attended the Christmas Ball at the Town Hall, but her parents had gone. Her mother had little to say about it the following morning, except to complain that the disco which had played for one half of the evening had given her a headache. Janna guessed that the sight of Colin spending the entire evening at the Morrises' table had also provoked her mother's discontent, but at least Mrs Prentiss had stopped openly complaining about this, and seemed to have resigned herself to the fact that Colin was now firmly attached to Beth.

Janna had not dared ask if Rian had been there with Kim San, but guessed from her mother's very reticence that he probably had been.

There were times when she wondered what course her life would have taken if it had been she and not her mother who had intercepted the post that fateful day seven years before, but she found the question almost too painful to contemplate.

Equally painful was the long article on Carrisbeck House which had appeared in the *Advertiser*, giving details of Rian's plans for the hostel and adventure courses that would be offered there. Janna had had to admit it was an excellent piece of public relations work—the tone of the article was thoroughly approving, and it revealed that the planned hostel had the backing of a well-known national foundation offering grants and awards for such schemes.

The next edition of the newspaper had carried a piece about Sir Robert and his opposition to the hostel, but this was fairly muted now, as if Sir Robert had to devote all his energies to sorting out the troubles at the engineering works, and had no time for such trivialities. Janna guessed that Rian would obtain his planning consent without too much trouble. Perhaps that was the only remaining barrier to his marriage with Kim San, she thought unhappily. He would want to know that he had a career locally to support his family with, and once permission was given for the hostel conversion, he would have few further problems.

She was standing in the market square a few days later, staring into a shop window, trying to find inspiration for some Christmas presents, when she felt a light touch on her arm. Turning, to her surprise she found Kim San smiling at her. It cost a great deal to return her greeting with any kind of warmth, but Janna managed it.

'You are better now?' the melodious voice asked. 'I have been so wishing to meet you, Miss Prent-iss. Fleur has told me of your many kindnesses.'

'It's nothing,' Janna protested awkwardly.

Kim San gave her a calm stare. 'It is a great deal,' she pronounced. 'This is a small town. I also come from a small town. In my town there are many warm hearts, but also some cruel tongues. I think the same may be true of this place.'

'Perhaps.' Janna gave a little shrug.

Kim San studied her perceptively for a moment, then smiled. 'It is very cold,' she said. 'Would you like to have some coffee with me?'

Janna hesitated, but she had no real reason to refuse. Besides, she was not proof against Kim San's gentle charm, so she agreed, imagining that they would go to the nearest café. But at that moment an all too familiar car drew up at the kerb beside them and Rian looked out through the driver's window.

'Oh, Ri-an,' Kim San greeted him. 'It is good that you have come. Here is Miss Prent-iss who will have coffee with us.'

Janna did not dare look at Rian. She could not meet his eyes. She stared down at the pavement wishing with all her heart that it would open and swallow her.

Silently he got out of the car and came and opened the doors for them. Fleur was bouncing around excitedly on the back seat.

'Oh, Miss Prent-iss!' she greeted Janna with something approaching rapture. 'Soon it will be Christmas. And next week I shall be in your play, and after that there will be the wedding. Will you be at the wedding, Miss Prent-iss?'

Janna wanted to reply, to say something light and amusing by way of excuse, but no words would come.

Kim San turned from the front seat and smiled at her. 'I hope you will come,' she said. 'We should be most pleased to see you there. Afterwards there will be a small party at the house—is that not so, Ri-an?'

'Yes,' he said shortly, and swung the car up the hill towards Carrisbeck House.

Janna shrank back against the seat murmuring something inadequate about not being sure of her plans, and was aware of Rian directing a cynical glance at her in the driving mirror.

Surely he couldn't expect her to be there? she thought wretchedly. Knowing how she felt about him—aware of his own feelings—he would not want to submit her to such an ordeal.

The car swept into the drive, and drew up before the front door. Kim San led the way up the steps, and Janna followed, feeling miserably that she was an interloper. She had hoped she would never have to set foot in this place again, or meet its master face to face, yet it seemed that she was to be spared nothing.

As she had once wished to be able to hate Fleur, she

now wished she could dislike Kim San, but it was impossible. She would have to be careful—so very careful—she told herself, not to give any of her secret thoughts away and dull the glow of Kim San's obvious happiness. Fortunately, she seemed to have no suspicion of the truth as she made the coffee and served it in the drawing room, which had now been additionally furnished with an ancient sofa of uncertain springs.

Kim San apologised for the bareness of the surroundings.

'It is well Ri-an did not warn me before I came of what it would be like,' she said with a pretty grimace. 'I think I would have stayed away until our apartment was finished. You have not seen our apartment, Jan-na, may I call you? It will be very nice, I think, when the furniture arrives next week.'

Janna tried desperately to think of an excuse not to look over the apartment, but nothing would spring to mind, and Kim San was already leading the way, delighted to have a guest to show over her future domain.

She was forced to admit that the conversion of the loft and stables seemed to have been a great success. The main living area had been given a blocked parquet floor, and most of one wall had been removed to make way for a huge picture window, giving an uninterrupted view over the dale. The worst moment came when she had to mount the wrought iron spiral staircase to the former loft to see the bedroom and bathroom which had been fitted almost miraculously into the available space. There was a private agony to be endured in looking into the larger of the two rooms, and knowing that was where Rian would sleep with Kim San.

'You look very pale, Jan-na,' Kim San gave her a searching look. 'Are you well?'

'Yes.' Janna loosened the top button of her shirt. 'It—it seems a little stuffy in here, that's all. I wasn't expecting any heating to be on.'

Kim San was all concern immediately, and led her out

into the fresh air. Janna could only be glad that Rian had not accompanied them, otherwise she was afraid she would have been bound to give herself away.

When they went back into the house, Fleur was in the drawing room practising 'Away in a Manger'.

'She sings so well,' Janna commented, glad to find a topic that had no personal connotations for herself.

'Yes,' Kim San acknowledged. 'Though it is too early to know if the voice will grow and develop or whether it is the talent of a child. In some ways, I hope that it is so.'

'You don't want her to be a singer?'

Kim shrugged. 'I want her to be happy,' she said quietly. 'Perhaps I think too much of my own experience. All I wanted to do was sing. I wished for nothing else.'

'But you don't feel like that now?' Janna asked.

Kim San shook her head. 'Now I wish to make a home for my child and my man. Years ago I could have done so, but I would not. I wished him to follow my career, and when he refused I quarrelled with him, and sent him away. I had the chance of fame—to appear on concert platforms all over the world. It seemed a great chance. Then I found I was to have his child, and I was angry. I demanded that he return to me and do as I wanted, and again he would not. He said I must come to him.'

'And so eventually you did,' Janna said, trying to smile.

'Yes,' Kim San agreed. 'But how many wasted years there have been between, and even now we are not together as I would wish. We have both changed, I know this, but perhaps we are wiser now, and I know we must take this chance to build our lives together.'

'Don't you hanker for your career, even now?'

Kim San shook her head. 'No,' she said calmly. 'I have another one now.'

She accompanied Janna to the front door, and shook hands smilingly, saying that she was looking forward to seeing her at the Nativity play. She obviously had no idea that Janna would be leaving the school, and was prepared to continue the friendship. If circumstances had only been different, Janna thought she would have liked to have had Kim San as a friend. But as things were, it was quite impossible.

She walked away down the drive, and paused as she reached the gates. Somewhere behind her she heard the purr of an engine, and saw the long sleek shape of Rian's car following her. She stood aside to let it pass, but he pulled up beside her.

'Get in,' he said shortly. 'I'll drive you back to town, or home, or wherever you're going.'

'No,' she burst out. 'I—I'd rather walk.'

'Don't lie,' he sent her a sardonic look. 'What you're really saying is that you don't want to drive with me.'

'If you know that, I don't know why you persist,' she said in a low voice.

'Frankly, neither do I,' he said coldly. 'I must have an inbuilt streak of masochism. Anyway, I'm not prepared to argue with you. Get in, Janna, before I make you.'

She hesitated. They were out of sight of the house, but if she ran, she knew he would come after her, and there would only be some kind of undignified scuffle. Setting her jaw, she walked round the car and climbed in silently.

He let in the clutch and moved off. She sat, her shoulders slightly hunched, as far away from him as she could get, a fact that wasn't lost on him, judging by the satirical smile that played around his lips.

'Relax,' he advised. 'You won't have to put up with my company for very long.'

'You don't make things very easy for me.'

'Have we ever made things easy for each other?' he asked coldly.

'No.' She moistened her lips. 'And I can't say I wasn't warned. When you wanted me with you, you told me what it would be like.'

He sent her a swift glance. 'How did you know about that?'

'My mother told me. She gave me your letter—only seven years late.' She tried a laugh, but it was a failure.

'And seven years too late,' he said almost conversationally. 'Don't worry about it, Janna. Pack it away among your souvenirs. I'm sure you must have some—I certainly have. Would you like to see one of them?'

He applied the brakes and brought the car smoothly to rest at the side of the road. He reached into an inner pocket and produced a small package loosely wrapped in tissue paper which he tossed into her lap. 'Remember this?'

Wonderingly, she unwrapped the flimsy paper covering and caught her breath. She was looking at a small white artificial rose, the sort of pretty ornament that a young girl might use to fasten in her hair at a party—a special party, anyway.

'It's a little crushed and faded,' Rian went on in the same almost casual manner. 'But then it's travelled a long way and been in some strange places.'

'I realised I'd lost it—that night,' she whispered. 'But I had no idea what had happened to it.'

'Well, now you do know,' he said abruptly. 'Have you nothing to say?'

'What can I say?' She shook her head helplessly, her eyes blinded by a rush of sudden tears. 'It makes no difference. How can it?' She drew a long, uneven breath. 'My God, you can be cruel!'

'That's rich coming from you.' He set the car in motion again, and Janna began to re-wrap the flower. He looked at her sharply.

'What are you doing?'

'Giving it back,' she said almost inaudibly.

'That's hardly appropriate under the circumstances,' he said with immense dryness. 'Keep it, sweet witch, or throw it away as you wish.'

'Don't you care?' she asked childishly.

'What has caring to do with it? As you reminded me so graphically the other day, I have no right to care. It was a salutory reminder, and I'm trying hard to live up to it. Hence the clearing out of old memories.'

She slipped the little bundle into her handbag with shaking fingers, hardly able to think coherently any more. The irony of the situation was almost more than she could bear. Only a few days before she had found that Rian had loved her all those years ago, loved her enough to want to marry her and take her with him in spite of pressures from his family. No wonder he had seemed bitter. Her lack of response to his letter must have convinced him that she was just playing some silly, childish game with him, pretending to love. His quarrel with his uncle and subsequent breach with his family must have seemed a totally futile action.

Yet in spite of this he had kept her rose, carried it with him as a reminder of her. And now at this moment, when they should have been closest, all the shadows fled and the ghosts laid, they had never been further apart. Kim San and Fleur were not ghosts. They were reality, and they deserved their chance for happiness. But for Kim San's insistence on her career, they would probably have been married years before, Janna told herself sombrely. In some ways she wished they had been, so that she would have at least been spared this heartache she was now suffering.

But he belonged to Kim San, just as surely as if the legal cermony had already been performed, she thought, and she had to crush down this bitter-sweet longing to feel his arms about her just once more.

As the car reached the bridge, she roused herself. 'Will you drop me here, please. I—I still have some messages.'

'As you please,' he said coolly.

She waited on the bridge until the car had disappeared, and then walked to the parapet and stood looking down into the lazily swirling water. The rose drifted down, the petals fluttering in the icy wind. Then the current took it, and it vanished under the bridge. Janna did not go to the other side to see if it reappeared. As she walked away, she felt that she had just let all the wildness and eagerness of her youth slip through her fingers for ever.

As the evening of the school concert and the Nativity play drew nearer, Janna felt herself growing increasingly nervous. She told herself that she had no logical reason for this. The rehearsals were going well, and Fleur's confidence was increasing daily. Janna was even able to ignore the sullen behaviour of Lucy Watson and her immediate circle.

She almost felt sorry for Lucy. She was a spoiled child, and she had obviously been convinced that Janna would be forced to change her mind about giving her the part when she learned what was being said.

Lucy now found her consolation in making the odd spiteful remark, which Fleur managed to appear never to hear, or at least to understand.

Inevitably, a rumour had got out that she was leaving, and several of the children showed an embarrassing disposition to hang around her, sighing mournfully. Janna was glad to have the Christmas preparations to take their minds off her imminent departure.

She had to pretend too that she did not know that money was being collected both by the children and the staff to buy her a leaving present.

Once as she sat at the back of the hall listening to a group of older juniors practising carols, she felt a lump come into her throat at the realisation that next Christmas she might be many miles away. She promised herself she would take the memory of this last week of term with its songs and parties and laughter and traditions with her, no matter how far she might travel. She smiled at herself rather sadly, thinking it was her disturbed emotions that were reponsible for that piece of sentimentality.

If she was sensible, she would take nothing with her from Carrisford—neither memories, nor regrets, nor frustrated yearnings.

She lived each day as it came, trying to look neither

forward nor back. She had spent too much of her life in retrospection, she told herself. If she started again now, she might find herself overwhelmed by might-have-beens.

The play and concert were due to be performed for the parents in the evening, and there was always a run-through in the afternoon, rather like a full dress rehearsal, watched by the infants department, an appreciative and uncritical audience who normally had a soothing effect on the frayed nerves of the young actors and performers.

The play was always the climax of the concert, followed only by a lusty mass rendering of 'O Come, all ye faithful' by everyone present.

The children were dressing for the play in a large classroom just near the hall. All the costumes had been taken home during the week and washed and pressed, and were now laid out carefully over desks while the wearers submitted gingerly to having a modicum of make-up applied. Janna was just finishing an artistic beard for one of the Wise Men, when she felt a tug at her sleeve. She glanced down and saw Fleur, very solemn and wide-eyed in vest and flowered knickers.

'You'd better get dressed,' she advised. 'There isn't very much time.'

'Come and look, Mees, please.' There was no gainsaying the urgent note in Fleur's voice, so with a slight sigh Janna abandoned a rather indignant shepherd who was waiting to have sixty years added to his age with the aid of a few greasepaint wrinkles, and went to see what was causing Fleur's concern.

The reason was not far to seek. The pale blue costume to be worn by the Virgin Mary was hung neatly across a chair, its pristine splendour destroyed for ever by the great smear of paint and glue which had appeared on the front.

Janna's lips parted in a gasp of dismay as she saw it. The little robe was utterly ruined. The glue that had been used was a brand which the children were always particularly careful not to get on their clothes because it was known not to wash out. The paint was just an added refinement.

Biting her lip, she picked the dress up and studied it to see if there was possibly enough material left undamaged to salvage for a makeshift costume, but there wasn't.

She was angry, but she had to mask her anger. She gave Fleur an encouraging smile. 'Well, you'll just have to wear that nice dress you had on earlier for now, and we'll think of something else for tonight. The infants won't mind.'

Fleur, little more than an infant herself in the school hierarchy, gave a solemn nod, but it was evident that tears were not too far away.

Janna did not bother to look at Lucy Watson. She knew there would be both guilt and triumph on her face, and she knew too that there was not a shred of proof. It could have been an accident, if the dress had not been folded carefully so that the smear was concealed until the wearer picked it up to put it on.

She could not accuse Lucy, but she did accuse herself of having underestimated the child's malice, although she suspected that the idea had been planted in her mind by someone older.

'Finish dressing, children,' she ordered calmly. 'I'll be back in a minute and I shall expect to find you all ready. No, Terry, I haven't forgotten your wrinkles and moustache, I'll do them when I come back.'

Vivien was in her office, and she waved a surprised hand at the phone when Janna said abruptly that she had to get in touch with Carrisbeck House.

Kim San answered, and Janna outlined in a few brief phrases what had happened, although she was careful to say it was an accident.

Kim San was reassuringly matter-of-fact. She was just about to go into town, she said. She would find some blue material and make another robe in time for the evening performance. She would bring it with her, she added, and that would ensure there were no more accidents.

Janna put down the phone with an uneasy feeling that

Kim San understood far more than she had given her credit for, and she hoped that none of the gossip that had been rife in the town only a short time before had reached her ears.

Vivien had been listening to one side of the conversation with pursed lips.

'An accident, eh?' she said, as Janna turned to go back to her cast. 'Someone just happened to be using paint and glue in the room where your kids were dressing. Come off it, Janna.'

Janna shrugged unhappily. 'What else could I say?'

'How about Lucy Watson?' Vivien propped her chin on her hand and gave her a wry look. 'They're not the most subtle family in town, you know, and they've been making no secret of their annoyance that she didn't get the part.'

Janna gave a sigh. 'So you've heard too, have you?'

'Oh, I've heard,' said Vivien. 'But I make a rule to believe half of what I see and nothing at all of what I hear. And the sort of rumours they've been spreading are just plain scurrilous. You haven't been letting them get to you, I trust?'

Janna paused, her hand on the door handle. 'A little,' she admitted ruefully. 'But I could take it. It's this—attack on Fleur herself that's sickened me.'

'Do you think it will affect her?'

'Time alone will show.' Janna glanced at her watch. 'Speaking of which, they're due on stage in two minutes. I must fly and do Terry's wrinkles.'

It could not be said that Fleur shone that afternoon. She was obviously very self-conscious about the fact that she was the only person on stage wearing everyday clothes, and her new confidence seemed badly shaken. She had difficulty in remembering her lines, and her small body was hunched and tense when the time came for her solo, with the result that she sang flat.

From the side of the stage, Janna saw Beth Morris exchange a covert grin with Lynn Carter who taught the reception class. If Fleur makes a mess of things tonight, Janna thought miserably, then people will start thinking there was some basis in the rumours after all, and that I didn't choose her simply because she seemed the best.

She gave no hint of this to Fleur or any of the children. She merely praised them all, and warned them to do just as well that evening, and to remember that shepherds and Wise Men never waved to their parents in the audience no matter how tempting it might seem.

Janna stayed behind for a while to help set out the remaining chairs that would be needed, and then walked slowly home for tea. The evening, she thought, was going to be pretty much of an ordeal, as broad hints had been dropped that her leaving presentation would take place after the concert, so that the parents could also join in expressing their appreciation to her. The Watsons, she thought with a touch of mordaunt humour, would probably boo and throw things.

She made herself put on the new dress she had bought for her holiday—champagne-coloured wool jersey, cut on empire lines with a round high neck and long sleeves—and she made up her face with unusual care, using blusher and eyeshadow meticulously. It was a braver face altogether that looked at her when she had done.

The hall was already half-filled when she arrived back at school. She went round to the classroom, and found the children busy getting ready, but not with the same *joie de vivre* that had been present that afternoon. Everyone seemed to be suffering from stage-fright to a greater or lesser degree, and even Lucy Watson was pale and silent.

Janna noticed with a small flutter of nervousness that Fleur was not among those present. Her heart sank as she wondered whether the child had been so unnerved by her failure that afternoon that she had decided not to appear in the evening. But even as she was asking herself whether she should put in another phone call to Carrisbeck House, Kim San's elegant little figure appeared in the classroom door-

way, leading Fleur by the hand. Janna gasped when she
saw her. In the limited amount of time at her disposal, Kim
San had performed wonders. The blue robe was perfectly
simple with its round neck and full sleeves, and a gold
dressing-gown cord made an effective girdle. The white
silky veil covered Fleur's hair and billowed almost to the
floor.

Kim San smiled with satisfaction at Janna's openly ex-
pressed admiration. 'When there is an emergency, one must
improvise,' was her only comment.

She looked round the room at the wide-eyed children.

'Which one is Lucy Watson?' she enquired. There was
a long pause, then Lucy stepped forward, bottom lip fixed
in a sullen pout.

'So you are Lucy.' Kim San studied her for a moment,
then smiled. 'How pretty, and you sing well, Fleur says. I
sing too, and if you would like, I will give you lessons—
when Christmas is over.'

Lucy's face was a study. Kim San gave her another,
rather enigmatic smile, added a wink for Janna's benefit
alone and departed.

Shortly afterwards the concert began. Janna could
register its progress by the bursts of applause which greeted
the end of each item, and she was able to gauge the moment when the curtains were drawn and she was able to get
her children to the hall and on to the stage with their
simple props.

From the moment that Jimmy Gordon, playing a Roman
centurion, unrolled his scroll and announced that all the
world was going to be taxed—a message greeted with rather
feeling laughter by some male members of the audience—
Janna knew the play was going to be a success.

The children's attack of butterflies had done them no
harm at all. Their adrenalin was obviously flowing, and
they threw themselves into the spirit of the play with
complete abandon. From the rough innocence of the shepherds to the majesty of the Wise Men, making their tradi-

tional entrance down the entire length of the school hall,
with nervous black slaves carrying the gifts for the Child
in front of them on cushions borrowed from home, they
captured the imaginations of their audience.

And when the moment came for Fleur, amazingly serene
like some exquisite porcelain figure, to kneel by the manger
and begin her solo, there were many adults in the hall
stealthily fumbling for handkerchiefs they had not suspected they would need.

Janna herself felt hot tears pricking at the back of her
eyelids as she listened. There was a talent there, she
thought, that could develop and grow if it was directed
with wisdom, and she knew that Kim San had that wisdom.
Janna could just see her, leaning forward slightly, the dark
almond eyes intent on her daughter's kneeling figure. Automatically her eyes moved to her companion, and she stiffened with astonishment. Rian was not there.

It was hard to believe he would not attend a school concert in which his own child was playing a leading role, she
thought bewilderedly. She looked towards the back of the
hall where some of the men were standing, to see if he was
among them, but his tall figure was nowhere to be seen.
She felt acutely disappointed in a strange way. She knew
now that Mrs Watson had not been so very far from the
truth. Whether she had been conscious of it or not, she had
hoped to please him tonight by presenting him with Fleur
at her best.

It was hurtful to wonder whether the rumours had in
fact got back to him, and if he had deliberately stayed away
because of them. Perhaps, after their parting on the bridge,
he simply did not wish to see her again. That was even
more hurtful to contemplate.

Afterwards when the final tableau had been staged, and
the curtain had fallen to tumultuous applause, Fleur came
to her starry-eyed. 'Oh, Miss Prent-iss, did you see? My
father is here, sitting with my mother.'

Janna shook her head compassionately. 'I don't think so,

dear,' she said quickly. 'I think something must have kept him away.'

'No.' Fleur gave her a puzzled look. 'He was there—I saw him. But I did not wave, Miss Prent-iss, because you said we must not.'

Janna collected herself with a start. 'Well, that was right, of course,' she said hurriedly. 'Now, everyone, into the hall for the final carol.'

When the last appeal to come and adore Him had died away, Mrs Parsons advanced to the front of the platform. Smilingly she thanked the audience for their attention, and the children and staff who had put on the concert. Then she paused.

'Many of you will be sorry to learn,' she said, 'that Miss Prentiss, whose first year junior class presented the play tonight, is leaving us this term. On your behalf I would like to present her with this travelling case, and this small clock which the children have chosen for her.'

Janna's eyes were unashamedly wet as she mounted the steps at the side of the stage and heard the applause. If there had been gossip—if the scandalmongers were sitting there that night—then it was all forgotten in the wave of warmth and interest and affection that Janna felt was almost tangible. She accepted her gifts, said a few stumbling words of thanks, and walked back into the body of the hall.

A number of parents approached her before leaving to express their regrets at her departure, and she smiled and thanked them and agreed that she, too, would miss Carrisford and its school.

She was just turning away when Kim San came up to her.

'What is this, Jan-na? You did not mention that you were to leave? I am sorry to hear this. Fleur is so fond of you.'

'And I'm fond of her too.' Janna forced a smile. 'But it's a mistake to stay in the same place for too long. You risk becoming staid—and stale. It's time I moved on.'

'You sound like Ri-an,' Kim San observed. 'Nothing will

do now than for him to leave again. He is so impatient. I have asked him to spend Christmas with us, but he will not.'

Janna stared at her. 'But it's your—first Christmas together!'

'That is what he says. He says he will be an intruder, but I say how can this be so, when he is our greatest friend?'

Janna began to feel bemused. It was an odd way, she thought, to refer to the man you were about to marry, even if the marriage was not wholly a love match.

'But surely he realises how much it will mean to Fleur to have him there?'

Kim San gave a wry smile. 'There would be little point in saying that when Ri-an knows quite well that he is no longer the first in her affections. Since her father came to us, he has been supplanted.'

'Her—father?' Janna did not know how she managed to utter the words.

Kim San gave her an odd glance. 'But yes. You did not know that he had come? He has been with us since yesterday. Come, you must meet him.'

She took Janna's unresisting hand and led her to where a tall, fair-haired man was standing.

'Philip, this is Janna Prentiss who has been Fleur's teacher.'

Janna looked dazedly up into a tanned face, firm-chinned and brown-eyed. Her hand was gripped warmly and firmly.

'I've heard a great deal about you, Miss Prentiss. I feel we have already met.'

'From Fleur, I suppose.' Janna struggled to gain her composure in a world that seemed to be reeling about her. Rian was Fleur's father, not this blond stranger.

He smiled down at her. 'Not entirely. I should tell you perhaps that I've been a friend of Rian's for over ten years. We started on the same paper together. I say, are you all right? You've gone quite pale.'

'Yes—yes, I'm fine,' Janna said mechanically. Her eyes sought Kim San's. The other girl was watching her, a gleam of understanding in her face. Frantically, Janna moistened her lips. 'You see—I thought ... I didn't realise ...' She stumbled to a halt, and Kim San gave a little smile.

'You thought that it was Ri-an I was to marry?' she asked on a soft note of incredulity, and Janna nodded.

Kim San shook her head. 'It explains much,' she said thoughtfully. 'But all Ri-an has ever been to me is a good friend. Philip and I might have remained apart for ever if it had not been for him. When he decided to turn his family home into an adventure school, it was Philip he thought of at once to take charge of it. Three years ago Philip gave up reporting to work as an assistant in such a school in Scotland. But there was no place there for me, and I was angry. Now, thanks to Ri-an, we have a home, and a job and a chance to be happy.'

'But—Rian let everyone think——' Janna began numbly, and paused.

'What they basically wanted to think,' Philip finished for her. 'It's a form of arrogance with him. But I think he would have explained had he been asked to by someone he —cared about.'

Janna's face was suffused with hot, painful colour under his considering look.

Kim San laid a gentle hand on her arm. 'Perhaps Ri-an too needs an explanation,' she said. 'But there is not a great deal of time. He is at the house now, packing.'

Philip produced a set of car keys and looked at her. 'Can you drive?' At her barely perceptible nod he tossed them to her. 'It's the blue station wagon parked just opposite the gates. We'll walk home—slowly.'

Janna found the vehicle without difficulty, and unlocked the door. She sat for a moment or two, forcing herself to be calm, wiping her suddenly clammy hands on a handkerchief. Then with infinite care she started the engine, and manoeuvred herself out of the parking space.

The now familiar shape of his car was missing from the front of the house, and everything seemed dark. With a feeling of agony, she thought, 'He's gone.' And at the same moment, she recognised that wherever he was, she would follow.

She got out of the station wagon and trod up the steps to the front door. She twisted the ornate handle and it yielded easily to her pressure and the door swung open with the faintest creak. Her heart lifted slightly. Surely he would not have driven away and left the house open like this, knowing that Philip and Kim San were at the school.

Like a ghost she flitted through the shadowed hall, less bare now with the addition of paper chains and holly, and started up the stairs. Instinct had guided her before. She let it take over again now, and it lead her to his old room, the one that Fleur now occupied.

It was dark, but she could see the faint outline of his tall figure at the window, and the glow of the cigar he was smoking.

She paused just inside the door. 'Rian,' she said, a little uncertainly.

He swung round with a muffled exclamation. The room was suddenly very still as if they had both ceased to breathe.

'What are you doing here, Janna?' he asked eventually. 'There's nothing for you here.'

'I haven't come to take,' she said steadily. 'I've come to give, if you'll let me.'

'Save your gift,' he said harshly. 'Save it for the man you're going to marry. I told you that once before. Travers still hankers after you, you know. You'd only have to lift your little finger to get him back.'

She shook her head, uncaring whether he could see her or not in the shadowy room.

'The gift is yours, Rian,' she told him. 'If you refuse me, then it will just have to remain ungiven for the rest of my life. There's no part of me that belongs to Colin—not even my little finger.'

She tried to laugh, but it ended in a sob. She heard him breathe her name, and then all darkness fled as his arms found her.

His mouth took hers with such hunger it was as if he was drinking heaven from her lips. The touch of his hands, the very pressure of his body against hers held a stark demand that she answered with totally joyous abandon.

'Oh, Janna, my sweet witch,' he murmured at last, his voice barely audible. 'I thought you'd settled for security as the lady of the manor the second time around. Your mother was so certain that it was Colin you really wanted. She told me if I had any real feeling for you that I'd get out of your life, and give you back your peace of mind. I didn't want to believe her, and then I saw how upset you were at that damned bazaar when he turned up with another girl.'

'That didn't upset me,' she protested, pressing her cheek against his chest and savouring the warmth of his skin through the thin wool sweater. 'I'd just discovered that everyone knew about that night we spent at the motel. One of the Watson girls works there and saw us. People were saying that I'd given Fleur the leading part in the school play because I was your mistress and wanted to please you.'

'I see,' he said drily. 'I suppose I should have explained more fully what the situation was when I brought Fleur here, but really I felt it was Kim San's and Philip's business, not mine. I came to Carrisford with Fleur to finalise matters over the house, and give those two a chance to sort out their problems on their own. They've had one parting and misunderstanding after another, but I always had the feeling that if they could just get together a while without any pressures that there might be a miracle. And I was in a position to offer some practical help as well, by turning Carrisbeck into an adventure school and offering Philip the chance of running it.'

He drew her over to the window and they sat down on the wide ledge that served as a window seat.

'You didn't want to live here yourself?' She traced the shape of his mouth with her forefinger.

'No. My memories of this house were never entirely happy. It's better that it should be used for some useful purpose. I think my uncle felt the same.' He paused. 'We made up our quarrel before he died. He didn't alter his will, but he drew up a deed of gift making over to me a sufficient sum to buy the house as soon as it came on the market. That's why I was able to act with such speed.'

'But you didn't have to do it all yourself,' she said. 'If your—memories were so unhappy, you could have appointed someone as your agent, surely?'

'I came back for you, Janna,' he said abruptly. 'I was hurt and bitter when you didn't answer my letter all those years ago, but no matter what I did—and God knows I tried—I couldn't forget you. You'd been my torment for long enough, so I decided I would make you suffer a little bit too. I guessed your conscience would still be troubling you over what happened all those years ago, and I told myself you'd asked for it.' He sighed. 'But then I saw you again, and it wasn't that simple any more. I saw the shell you'd built up around yourself, and I had to find out if you—the real you—were still there inside it. As soon as I kissed you, I knew that you were, and I knew also that I had to have you, even if I had to fight dirty to get you.' He kissed her lingeringly. 'I told myself it just wasn't possible you could love Travers and respond to me as you did. But when you broke with him, suddenly I was at a distance again.'

'I thought you were going to marry Kim San,' she told him candidly.

'Following on, I suppose, from the burning conviction in everyone's mind that I had to be Fleur's father.' He gave a slight chuckle. 'I never actually said I was, you know. But I guessed that whole numbers of people, your worthy headmistress among them, were leaping to conclusions from the few details I felt able to give.'

'But you could have told me.'

He kissed her again. 'You never asked me, my love, or

I would have done. And when I thought that it was Colin you really loved after all, I told myself you hadn't asked because you didn't care.'

'I cared,' she whispered against his lips. 'Oh, God, how I cared! I—I gave in my notice at school, because I couldn't bear the thought of having to live in the same town and know that you were there, married to someone else.'

'My own feelings were practically identical.' He gave an unsteady laugh. 'And I blame other people for leaping to conclusions. What a pair of fools we've been!' His arms tightened around her. 'But it's over now. We don't have to suffer any more, either of us. Don't you realise, my darling, we're both free, to go anywhere we want—together.'

'Just as though the last seven years had never happened,' she whispered with a catch in her voice. 'Oh, Rian, where shall we go?'.

'Wherever my work sends me,' he said simply. 'Nothing has changed. It will still be the same life in hotels, living out of suitcases, that I offered you before. But this time, I promise you, we'll make a permanent home—to bring our children up in. But not yet. I'll want you all to myself for a while at least.'

He bent his head and their lips met in a passionate kiss that wiped away all the bitterness of the past, and made the future a shining reality.

As they clung to each other, in the distance a child's voice began to sing 'Away in a Manger', a pure sound with an almost unearthly sweetness as it floated up to them through the still winter air.

Rian raised his head. 'Fleur,' he said with a laugh in his voice. 'A tactful way of telling us we're no longer alone. Shall we go down and tell them?'

He kissed her again, then hand in hand they went out of the room together.

Take your holiday romance with you

Mills & Boon

Accept 4
Best Selling Romances
Absolutely
FREE

Enjoy the very best of love, romance and intrigue brought to you by Mills & Boon. Every month Mills & Boon very carefully select 4 Romances that have been particularly popular in the past and re-issue them for the benefit of readers who may have missed them first time round. Become a subscriber and you can receive all 4 superb novels every month, and your personal membership card will entitle you to a whole range of special benefits too: a free monthly newsletter, packed with exclusive book offers, recipes, competitions and your guide to the stars, plus there are other bargain offers and big cash savings.

As a special introduction we will send you
FOUR superb and exciting
Best Seller Romances – yours to keep Free
– when you complete and return
this coupon to us.

At the same time we will reserve a
subscription to Mills & Boon Best Seller
Romances for you. Every month you will
receive the 4 specially selected Best Seller
novels delivered direct to your door. Postage
and packing is always completely Free.
There is no obligation or commitment -
you can cancel your subscription
at any time.

You have absolutely nothing to lose and a whole world of
romance to gain. Simply fill in and post the coupon today to:-
MILLS & BOON READER SERVICE, FREEPOST,
P.O. BOX 236, CROYDON, SURREY CR9 9EL.

Please note:- READERS IN SOUTH AFRICA write to
Mills & Boon Ltd., Postbag X3010,
Randburg 2125, S. Africa.

- - - - - - - - - - - - - - - - - - - -

FREE BOOKS CERTIFICATE